Begi

~

Dee Mann

Mason Marshall Press
Medford, Massachusetts

This book is a work of fiction. Names, characters, places, and incidents are entirely the product of the author's imagination or are used fictitiously and are not to be construed as real. Any resemblance to actual events, locales, organizations, persons, or anything else is entirely coincidental

Published by Mason Marshall Press

For information, please contact:

Mason Marshall Press
P.O. Box 324
Medford, MA 02155

ISBN-13: 978-1-63247-049-2

PRINTED IN THE UNITED STATES OF AMERICA

Many thanks are owed to Martha, Bernadette, Rhoda, and Joe for their eagle eyes, excellent suggestions, and encouragement.

Thanks! Thanks!

Dee

Contents

Coffee Girl

Keri glanced at the clock, muttering under her breath about the unfairness of life. It was bad enough her roommate told her this morning he was moving out and in with his girlfriend who she knew was so absolutely wrong for him. Now she would have to start interviewing new potential roommates, though she knew she would never find anyone who made her feel the way Gary did when he looked at her, or smiled, or laughed, or had milk dripping down his chin in the morning. And to top it all off, Phil called in sick this morning so, in addition to the espresso machine, she was stuck tending the brewers that kept the twelve carafes of coffee full for the rush of college kids and power suits who were all too important and too busy to have to wait for anything, much less a caffeine fix.

At least I don't have to smile and make nice with them. Small blessings, I guess.

She would not have believed it possible when she started the job, but after three months, she knew most of the regulars by sight and many of their names and what they usually ordered. By the end of her sixth month, which was last week, the 'many' became nearly all. When she was not in a foul mood, she enjoyed the give and take with the customers, the little jokes, and smiles. And the tips were tremendous.

She dumped the used grounds and added freshly ground almond vanilla-creame beans to the brew funnel. As she pressed the start button, she heard, "Excuse me" and looked around at a new face.

"I'm sorry to bother you, but the Colombian decaf is empty. No rush. There was a little left in the decanter thing. I'm over in the corner by the window. Whenever it's ready would you please let me know. Or just throw something at me to get my attention."

He grinned and it was the kind of grin that was so genuine Keri automatically returned it, despite her mood. "I'll let you know," she said, all the while thinking, *Sorry to bother you? No rush? Please? What planet did this guy fall to Earth from?*

Despite her mocking thoughts, she realized her mood had lightened and glanced his way. He was hunched over a laptop, furiously typing away. She wondered if he was a student or some tech guy or maybe a writer of some kind as she dumped the decaf beans into the grinder before punching up the next espresso order, a large latte with extra foam and a dusting of cocoa powder.

When the decaf was ready, he was still focused on his laptop. For a second, she toyed with the idea of balling up some napkins and throwing them at him as he requested, but instead, poured him a large cup.

"Oh! Thank you!" he said when she set the cup down next to him. "You didn't have to bring it to me. I can see how busy you are."

"That's okay. It'll do some of them good to slow down and wait an extra minute or two. I didn't know how you take it so I left room for milk or cream."

"Black is perfect. When I want coffee-flavored something, I buy ice cream." Again his grin was rewarded with one in return. "Thank you again. It was very nice of you."

By ten-thirty, the morning madness slowed to the normal steady stream and Keri took her break. She sipped a hot chocolate while explaining to Cathy, the owner, cook, and baker, why Gary's girlfriend would only hurt him in the end.

"Have you told *him* any of this?"

"No! I could never. He'd just think I was jealous or desperate or something."

"Right. Or something. How about some truth. He shared that place with you for over a year before he met what's-her-name. You had your chance and you let it slide."

"But I wanted *him* to want *me*."

"Bah. Men don't know what the hell they want. We have to hit them over the head. Did you ever compliment him on whatever manly thing he was up to at the moment? Did you ever dress so he'd notice you? Or better yet, let him get an accidental peek at you in your underwear? Hell, you were living with the guy. You had every opportunity, girl."

"Oh good lord," Jan said as she came through the door from the front. "Is she still going on about Gary? She's been muttering under her breath all morning. We're out of M&M cookies. And who's the geek in the corner you played waitress with earlier?"

Keri shook her head and sighed. "He's nobody. He was just nice and polite during the rush instead of biting my head off because the decaf was empty, so I brought him a cup of coffee when it was ready. Did you recognize him?"

"No. First time I've seen him here. Polite, huh? We could certainly do with more of that around here in the morning."

Steve One and Steve Two were partners in a small insurance business and served as the shop's lunch-rush early warning system. They walked in at eleven-twenty every morning to get their lunches. By the time whatever sandwiches they ordered were ready, the line at each station would be growing.

For, perhaps, the hundredth time, Keri wondered how anyone could be so consistently punctual. She imagined people in the surrounding buildings watching for them, setting off an ever-increasing circle of customers as people saw others leaving for lunch.

The Steves were still placing their order and the line was already growing. Had Cathy not offered to pay double-time to convince Tom T. to come in and help with the lunch rush, to say it would have turned into a zoo would have been a colossal understatement. It would have been much closer to a wild animal park.

By one-thirty, customers slowed to a trickle and Keri had time to breathe again. She checked the corner table but found it empty and regretted not going over to talk with him during her morning break.

If he's new in town, or here on business of some sort, he might appreciate...what? What's wrong with you? Now you're mooning over a stranger who was polite. Good grief, girl, get a grip!

Keri was beat by the time her apartment door closed behind her. All she wanted was to languish in a hot bath with a glass of wine. She dropped her bag on the chair and froze. Something was off. She was sure of it, but could not tell what. She looked in the kitchen but everything appeared fine until she noticed the gap on the counter.

"Ohmygod, Gary's espresso machine. It's gone. We've been robbed!"

She raced to her bedroom but nothing seemed to be missing. Her jewelry box was untouched as were the few pieces she hid in her underwear drawer.

What the hell?

She crossed the living room to Gary's room, pushed the partially opened door, said, "Oh damn!" and turned to get her cell phone from her bag.

When he answered, she said, "What the hell, Gary?"

"What?"

"All your stuff is gone."

"I told you I was moving in with Elise."

"That's right. This morning. At five AM. And ten hours later…what did you do, spend all day packing and moving?"

"Pretty much. We're in love, Keri. I wanted to be with her. You should be happy for me."

"I'll be happy when I find another roommate I can live with without wanting to pull my hair out."

"Speaking of which, there's an envelope in the freezer with my share of next month's rent. If you find someone before the end of the month, use it…well, for whatever. Buy yourself something nice"

"Why is it in the freezer?"

"Because I figured when you realized I was gone, if you couldn't get me on the phone, you'd go for the Cherry Garcia."

"You jerk. Hold on."

When she opened to freezer door, there it was, propped against the ice cream.

"You could have told me you were leaving today instead of running out like some deadbeat tenant." She tore open the envelope.

"Come on, Ker. You know I'm no good with goodbyes."

"Hey, this check is ten dollars short."

"I know. That's the ten bucks you owe me from the bet."

"Bet? What bet?"

"Are you kidding? About six weeks after I moved in, remember? We were doing tequila shots and watching some sappy movie you picked and we bet ten dollars on who would fall in love first. I won!"

"No you didn't you jerk. I won. I was already in love with *you*!"

"What? Keri! What?!"

Oh shit! Oh shit! Nice going girl.

"Relax, Gary. I was just messing with you. You always were too easy. Look, I wish you and her the best of luck. Stop in the shop some day soon and I'll buy you both a coffee. But I have to go now. I have an ad to write."

~ ~ ~

"You look like crap," Cathy said when Keri walked into the back for an apron.

"Gary moved all his stuff out yesterday while I was here."

"Ohhh. I'm sorry, Keri. But maybe it's for the best." She didn't ask if the way she looked was from crying, insomnia, getting sick on ice cream, or all three.

"Yeah. Maybe." She headed out front to start setting up for the day.

Just before eight, Keri came out of the back with a customer's breakfast wrap when she saw the polite guy from yesterday standing in Phil's line. Their eyes met and she smiled as he grinned and nodded. She rang up the sale and when she looked up again, saw he moved to her line.

"Good morning," he said when he reached the counter. "Are you okay? You look…ill?"

"Good morning. I'm fine. Just a little…a lot of insomnia last night. What can I get you?"

He placed his order and as she put it together, she found herself resisting the urge to look back over her shoulder at him. And when it was ready, he handed her a ten, then stuffed the four dollars and twenty-seven cents change in her tip jar.

The morning crowds thinned early, so she let Phil take his break first. When it was her turn, she took a hot chocolate and a large decaf over to the table in the corner where the new guy sat typing.

"Hey! Coffee girl. What's this?"

"This is my thank you for that tip earlier," she said, placing the coffee on the table, "but you realize it was much too much for a coffee and a couple of muffins."

"Nonsense. I used to wait tables when I was in college and the experience made me a generous tipper. Especially when there's a pretty girl involved."

She felt color rising in her cheeks. "Oh dear. I was going to ask if I could join you for a few minutes, but now I'm not sure if I'd be sharing a table with a masher or someone with terrible eyesight."

"I assure you I'm neither," he said with a laugh as he closed the cover of the laptop and waved her to a chair across the table. "I'm Efrem, but my friends call me EZ."

"As in easy to talk to?"

He laughed. "No. As in Efrem Zimbalist Jackson. My mother is a huge fan of old TV shows. She loves this actor Efrem Zimbalist Jr. and so when I was born, I got named after him."

"Wow. That's a great story! And a cool nickname. I'm Keri Watson. My friends call me…Keri."

"So, to what do I owe the honor of sharing your break time? Beside the tip, of course."

"Well, beside the tip, it was how nice you were yesterday morning. Customers around here are always in a hurry and usually get a little testy when they have to wait for their coffee to brew. Plus…well, a polite new person who hangs around the shop working is quite the rarity, so everyone's a little curious about you."

"Everyone?"

"Ummm..okay, not everyone. Me. But they will be now that I'm sitting here talking to you. So don't tell me anything you don't want everyone in the shop to know."

"I see. Was it my rugged good looks, my obvious intelligence, or my irresistible sex appeal that drew you here?"

"Actually, it was your manners."

"Ouch! I guess mom would be happy to hear that, but my ego wants to run and hide."

Keri laughed as he play-acted despair. "I was kind of in a foul mood yesterday morning and you being so unexpectedly polite really lifted my spirits. And then this morning you were all like, 'good morning' and smiling and happy despite how I must have looked and it helped again. So I got curious and here I am."

"Hmmm…are these foul moods and sleepless nights a common occurrence?"

"No. My roommate moved out yesterday and I was bummed. So what do you do on the computer?"

"Do you want the long version or the short?"

She glanced at the clock. "I have ten minutes left of my break."

"Short version it is, then. I do systems analysis. Basically, I study something and figure out if it can be made better and how to do it if it's possible."

"Wow. What are you working on now?"

"Sorry. I can't discuss clients or what I do for them, but if you want an example, turn around and take a look at how the store is set up, particularly, the pastry racks. Do you see any way to improve efficiency there?"

She stared at them for a minute then turned back and

shrugged. "It works fine the way it is."

"I'm sure it does, because everyone is used to it. Look again. Now, I know that blueberry is the most popular muffin choice because you keep two trays on the racks."

"Right. So?"

"You have three service stations. Call them one, two, and three, left to right. When a customer orders a blueberry muffin at station three, the server turns around, takes one or two steps, and can bag or plate the muffin. But if a customer at station two, in the middle orders one, the server has to take three or four steps. And from station one, the server has to take five or six steps to get a muffin.

"Now, if you had one tray of those muffins on each side, the server at station one would save six or eight steps on every blueberry muffin order. And the server in the middle would have a choice, so if number three server is getting a muffin, he can go to the tray on the other side, saving a few seconds.

"That's just one example. If your boss hired me to streamline the serving process, I'd study sales records and figure out the optimum spot for each item." He grinned and raised his eyebrows. "Suggest the muffin thing to your boss and try it out for a week. Who knows, you might get a raise."

He was pleased to see she caught on immediately and questioned him about other possibilities in the few minutes left of her break.

"Thank you! After the lunch rush, I'll tell Cathy and the others about it."

"Make sure you take the credit. If word gets out I'm giving advice for free, my hourly rate is going to take a nosedive."

He watched her walk away thinking, *nice smile*, then, *nice butt, too* before sipping his coffee and returning to his keyboard.

~ ~ ~

The next morning, he grinned after his 'good morning' and nodded at the two trays. "How's it working?"

"You were right. It's amazing. It saves ten or twelve seconds from this station."

"There you go."

"Want your usual?"

He nodded. "And I hope you'll join me on your break again."

"I will, thanks." She handed him the cup and placed the plate with two muffins on the counter.

When he reached into his pocket, she held up her hands and said, "Nope. It's on the house today." And when he opened his mouth to argue, she said, "Boss's order. You want me to get in trouble?"

Keri began spending all her morning breaks at his table as well as her afternoon breaks when he was still there after the lunch rush. By Friday, she learned he expected to be in town for six or eight more weeks, his home address was his parents' house but he had not been back there for nearly nine months, and that he lived in hotels or short-term rental apartments, whichever was provided by the client.

By the end of the second week, they had discussed a long list of personal preferences including colors, sandwiches, movies, ice cream, and philosophers.

~ ~ ~

The following Tuesday, Gary and Elise came in to say hello. Keri bought them coffee, as promised, and during the five minutes they chatted, got the distinct impression the visit was Elise's idea.

Later, when she mentioned it to EZ, he suggested Elise might not have believed she and Gary were just roommates and wanted to see how he reacted around her.

~ ~ ~

Three days later, EZ asked her out.

"Honestly, Keri, unless I'm sleeping or talking to you on one of your breaks, I've been working, and it's starting to wear me down. I need a break and you're the only non-client type person I know here so I was wondering if you would like to go see a movie or go bowling or anything that'll get me out of the hotel room for a few hours. Strictly platonic, as friends. I'll even pay. Or not. Whatever you want. You can even pick the movie. What do you say?"

She was impressed with how nicely he begged without actually begging. "Well, I'd planned on finally putting the ad for a new roommate on Craigslist tonight, but I suppose it can wait until the morning."

They made plans to meet in front of the shop at seven and walk to the multiplex.

"Good lord," he said as they walked out of the theater. "Please explain to me what you — what women — like so much about those kinds of movies."

"Hey, *you* wanted me to pick the movie. Even when I demurred, you insisted. So I picked what looked like a nice rom-com. To tell you the truth, it was a little gross at times, but I guess that's what kids like these days."

He laughed. "Kids? You're just a kid yourself. What are you, all of twenty-two, twenty-three?"

She threw her head back and slapped her hand over her heart. "Oh, I love you for saying that. Say it again. Please?"

"What? That you look like you're twenty-two or twenty-three?"

"Thank you, EZ. I knew there was a reason I came and sat with you the first time. It was so I could hear that. But the truth is, I turned twenty-seven two months ago."

"I would have bet money against that. I'm thirty, by the way. In case you were wondering."

"I was, actually. But I would have asked you Monday.

"I had a really good time, EZ. Thanks. But I'm working tomorrow and five AM is not all that far away. Would you mind waiting with me at the stop up there until the bus comes?"

"Bus? Are you nuts? I'm not letting you take a bus home."

Despite her protestations, he flagged a taxi, insisted on paying the driver in advance, and included a generous tip to make sure she got in her building safely.

~ ~ ~

"He actually said that to a taxi driver in *this* city?" Cathy asked.

"Seriously. And he must have tipped him pretty well because the guy watched me until I opened the front door and walked in. When I got up to my apartment, I looked out the window half-expecting him to still be there, waiting for the lights to go on."

"Well, well. This guy sounds like a keeper."

"Sure, for another month or two at best. Then he's off to his next job."

"Such a shame."

Keri shrugged. "That's my luck. One way or another, they always leave. At least this time, I know he's leaving, so he won't be taking part of my heart with him. If I can't have a relationship, at least I can have a good time for a couple of months."

She saw Cathy's eyebrows shoot up and added, "No. Not that kind of good time. He made that clear yesterday. And to be honest, I'd rather be the friend he had fun with while he was here than just be the girl he screwed for awhile."

Keri got her wish. The next five weeks were filled with conversations during the day and fun around town most nights. Despite her promise to herself to keep it all friendly and safe, she found herself longing to sit with him when she was working and fighting the urge to hold his hand or put her arm around him when they were walking. She knew she was falling for him a little, but it was just a little, and the knowledge he would leave soon and she would never see him again helped keep her heart safe.

~ ~ ~

No sooner did she plop down for her morning break than he asked, "Is there any chance you could get two or three days off at the end of the week?"

"Umm, I don't know. What's going on?" As soon she asked the question, his expression betrayed the answer. "Oh."

"I'll be done on Wednesday, but my flight to Paris isn't until Sunday evening. Please, don't look so sad."

"I'm sorry. I knew you'd be leaving soon. It just took me by surprise."

"Don't apologize. I guess I feel the same way. Look, I've been doing this work for five years and I've been in a lot of coffee shops and hung out with a lot of people, guys and girls. But I've never enjoyed myself more than I have here, with you. In many ways, you and I are kindred spirits and in other ways, so different. But hanging out with you was easy and always fun, even when we argued about stuff like those god-awful movies you dragged me to. You're the best friend I ever made on a job and all because my momma taught me to be polite. Can you imagine? Anyway, I'll have three and a half days free before I leave, and I'd really like to spend as much of the time as I can with you. Whatever you want to do. In town, out of town, go somewhere for a few days, it doesn't matter. What do you say?"

She said yes, of course, even though she knew it would make his leaving that much harder.

~ ~ ~

It would have been a whirlwind romance if romance had been the endpoint. Instead, it was a whirlwind goodbye, packed with laughter and fun and long conversations and the joy of just sharing time with a wonderful friend she would probably never see again.

And then he was gone.

On the way home from the airport, she convinced herself she was not going to cry, but when she closed her apartment door and collapsed on the sofa and thought about that final hug goodbye, how could she not.

~ ~ ~

In the weeks after EZ's departure, Keri threw herself into working. She decided her homage to EZ would be to find ways to make the shop more efficient. And she did. With Cathy's help, she compiled sales data and took the muffin-tray trick to the next level, rearranging the trays in the racks and display cases to put the biggest sellers within easy reach of the staff. Then she delved into coffee sales, impulse items, and even came in on a day off to study how the shop looked from the customer's perspective. And five weeks after he left, she got a surprise that banished the rest of the blues.

When Cathy called her into the office, Keri wondered if she went too far, disrupted things too much.

Oh, well. I'll find out in a minute.

"I know you started with the efficiency thing to give yourself something to focus on so you wouldn't be thinking about an absent friend. I didn't think it would accomplish much, but I figured it would be good therapy for you. Well, I just closed out the books for last month and I thought you might be interested in what I discovered."

"Oh lord, don't tell me I did all that for nothing."

"Okay, I won't tell you that. Instead, I'll tell you that sales are up almost ten percent from the month before. We're selling more of everything because we're serving more customers faster. Lines move faster so people don't pass us by when they are long. Even the average sale amount is up, probably thanks to the impulse displays."

"That's great news!"

"Yes, it is. And this is for you." She handed Keri an envelope and watched her reaction as she opened it.

"That's fifty percent of the increased profit. It was all your doing and you deserve it. Now give it back."

"What?"

"Give it back and I'll explain."

Bewildered, Keri passed the check back.

"Did you know I opened this business because I love to bake?"

Keri shook her head.

"Well, I did. If I thought I could make a go of it here just selling baked goods, I'd do it in a minute. But it's the coffee that really brings them in. Here's another thing I bet you don't know. I hate working the front. I hate managing the front. I hate thinking about the front. I'd much rather put my time and thought into coming up with new, delicious things to eat. But I never could. Then I got an idea. I should hire someone to run the front for me."

Huh? Is she…

"Are you talking about promoting me to a manager or something?"

"That was my first thought. You've always been the best employee here, so you would have been the natural choice for a manager."

"Would have been?"

"Right. If I was hiring a manager. But managers are

just, well, managers of something someone else owns. No manager will ever devote herself to a business the way an owner would. You can see that, right?"

"Right. So you're *not* offering to make me a manager?"

"Correct. I want you to be my partner." She held up the check. "And this can be your down payment."

~ ~ ~

Keri sat in EZ's former seat watching two guys with jackhammers dig up the sidewalk across the street as she thought about her first month as an owner. When she said yes to Cathy's proposal, she had no idea just how much work was involved. Schedules, books, ordering, vendors — she was amazed Cathy found time to do it all and still keep the pastry shelves full. But now that she had her first taste of business, she could not imagine ever wanting to go back.

She closed her eyes and listened to the sounds of a busy shop. Customers ordering or talking on their phones or at the tables, display case doors sliding, lattes being foamed, coffee brewing; it was all a symphony of sorts, one she had come to love.

Her cell phone rang, and for the dozenth time, she regretted giving it to all the vendors. She didn't recognize the number. *Probably another one trying to sell us something.*

"Hello?"

"If I timed this correctly, you're on your break, yes?"

"Yes. But who is this?"

"Ahhh! You don't recognize my voice?"

"I…hold on." She jumped up and headed for the Ladies' Room. "Okay. There was lot of background noise and I couldn't hear well. Say something now."

"Something now."

She rolled her eyes. "More than that if…wait…EZ?

Is that you?"

"Thank goodness. My ego was in a death spiral for a minute there. How are you doing, coffee girl?"

"I'm great. I miss our talks, but things have been going really well for me. How about you? How's Paris?"

"Okay, I guess. I did the tourist thing a couple of weekends, but mostly I'm working. I did find a nice coffee shop, but it's not the same."

"Well, what did you expect? Nobody makes coffee like we do."

"That's not what I meant."

Keri's stomach flipped and she closed her eyes and told herself, *Don't. He's just being polite. Keep it light.* "Surely it's not the muffins."

"No. To tell the truth, it was those *terrible* movies you dragged me to."

She laughed. "They were not terrible. You just can't appreciate the finer nuances of chick flicks."

It was his turn to laugh but when he spoke again, it was with his serious voice.

"Keri, something happened yesterday. Something sort of out of the blue. And maybe it's a good thing and maybe not. I'm not sure yet. But it's serious and I know we were just friends for a few months but you always told me what you thought, good or bad, and I need to talk to a woman about this, someone who'll tell it to me straight, not just what she thinks I want to hear. Are you up for that?"

"EZ, please tell me you're not really sick or something."

"No, it's nothing like that. But it could change my life. Serious stuff."

"Okay, then tell me. No, wait. I'm standing in the bathroom. Hold on."

In the space of half-a-minute, she explained things to Cathy, who smiled and said, "Close the door and if you absolutely must put your feet on the desk, take your shoes off first."

"Okay, EZ. I'm in the office. Now what's going on?"

"I got a call yesterday from a company that apparently liked the work I did for them so much they want me to come work for them full-time. I'd be working from the home office, only occasional traveling, pretty much be my own boss, and crazy money and benefits."

"Wow! It sounds fantastic. But if you're calling me, I'm guessing you're not sure if you should take it?"

"Exactly. I kind of like what I do now. A few months here, a few months there…the job has let me see an awful lot of the world."

"But?" She heard him sigh.

"But I meet a lot of people, get close to some of them for awhile, like I did with you, then I'm gone, usually never to return. I don't really have any friends, Keri, not even friends like you and the other people at the shop are."

"So you're lonely?"

"A little. Maybe. Sometimes. But it's not just that. What makes the job offer most attractive to me is that, well, when I was working there, I…I met someone."

Again her stomach flipped and again her better judgment said, *Don't do it. It's someone else. That's why he's calling me.*

"We had a really good time together while I was there, but we both knew I'd be leaving. The thing is, I kind of developed feelings for her, you know? Not that I ever told her. It wouldn't have been fair to her. And as you know, I'm much too polite to be unfair."

Keri could tell from his voice they were sharing a grin.

"So here's the problem. As much as I like what I'm doing now, I've realized recently that I've been missing her. And what it comes down to is that if I thought she had developed feelings for me, too, I'd take the job."

"So tell her how you feel."

"Sure. I call her up and say what? Gee, I know we had fun when I was there, but I'm thinking of moving there permanently but only if you're as hot for me as I am for you because I want to settle down and fall in love and get married and have kids and…and do you see the problem?"

She did. It wasn't her he wanted. But that was her problem.

"Look, EZ, the only way you'll find out if she likes you the way you hope is to ask her. But you can't do it on the phone. You have to face her so she can see how serious you are and you can see her reaction. When do you have to let these guys know about the job?"

"The week after this job is done. About a month from now."

"Then, when the job's done, come back and talk to her. Tell her how you feel, tell her everything, and hope she feels the same way."

"You're sure?"

"You wanted the truth. There it is."

They chatted for awhile, reliving good times, bad movies, and bowling balls thrown backwards until both had to get back to work.

Keri sighed as she opened the office door.

"Sooooo?" Cathy said with a hopeful look on her face.

"Basically, he wanted to know how to tell some girl he likes her and find out if she likes him."

"Oh." The hopeful look turned to sadness. "I thought maybe…"

"Me, too. Oh, well. Want me to take the tray of cookies out?"

The Steves walked through the front door as she came out of the back with the tray. "Hi, guys. I'll be with you in a minute."

Geez, twenty past already. It didn't seem like we were talking that long.

"I've got them," she heard Phil say as she bent down to slide the tray of cookies into the display case. "Want to check the coffees?"

She stood and stretched just as a loud voice asked, "Do you folks still have table service here?"

She turned toward the sound, scanned the tables, and did a double-take, her eyes wide with disbelief. "EZ? EZ!" She dashed from behind the counter. "What are you doing here? Why didn't you…oh. Oh! You mean you…all the time you were…?"

She took a breath, looked around to see who might be watching, and sat down. "It's nice to see you again. What brings you here?"

He smiled. "You know why I'm here."

"I'm sure I don't."

Two can play at this game. Ohmygod, two can play. Two!

His smile broadened. "I see. Well, I've missed you since I left. I've missed you a lot. Your smile. Your sassy attitude. Your single-handed support of the hot chocolate industry. I've missed all of you, Keri. And I have an opportunity to move here permanently. But I've realized it would be too difficult to live in the same town as you without you. So I've come to find out if you have any feelings for me at all beyond friendship. Because what I feel for you goes way beyond that."

"Is that so? How far beyond?"

"You're really going to make me work for this, aren't you?"

She picked up his cup for a sip and was surprised to

find lukewarm hot chocolate. She was glowing as she set the cup down, but just smiled and raised her eyebrows and waited.

"Keri Ann Watson, it is my hope that the feelings I have for you, and any feelings you may have for me, will one day grow and lead to a life together filled with love, and togetherness, and someday marriage and children and a home with a yard and maybe even a dog. I don't know how it happened, but it did. A part of you has become a part of me. And now I find I want…I need the rest of you to make me whole. That's how far beyond."

When his voice died, Keri realized there was no background noise in the shop. She turned to find everyone in the store watching them and felt her cheeks grow hot again, but she didn't care. She turned back to face him and said, "Efrem Zimbalist Jackson, you really must have been blind not to see how I felt about you months ago. Hugging you and watching you leave was the hardest thing I've ever done. And I have no idea why I'm going on like this when what I really want to say is that I'm very, very happy you took my advice.

"Now take *me* please and don't *ever* let me go."

The Watcher

Sasha skipped down the stairs, wondering if he would be there.

Six months previous, she noticed him watching her from the center platform. Had he not been so well dressed, right down to shoes polished to a shine she could see from across the tracks, she might have assumed him some kind of weirdo from the way he just stared at her. She buried her nose in her Kindle that day, but could not stop herself from periodically checking to see if his eyes were still on her. They were. Each time. And when the train arrived, she watched him watching her as she entered the car and took her seat. She wondered if he would speak to her when he entered and received her answer when he turned and walked to the following car.

Okay, so he is a weirdo.

As the subway cars rattled through the dark tunnels, she worried he might get off at her station. What would she do? What *could* she do? But when the train arrived at her stop, he was nowhere to be seen.

The next morning, she decided to simply ignore him, but she didn't have to. He wasn't there. She thought about him once that evening, on the ride home, but by Monday, forgot all about him.

Three days later, as she swiped her card and pushed through the turnstile, she cursed her decision to wear her new heels. They looked so great on her when she bought them. Who knew they would turn into implements of torture.

Maybe I should have walked around in them for a while first.

She took the stairs slowly to minimize the discomfort, then made her way onto the platform. Her thoughts were on her toes and how quickly the shoes would come off once she reached her office. She thumbed her Kindle's power switch, anxious to learn if Dirk really was the illegitimate son of a shipping magnate and if Rosalind would give him her heart or cast him aside for his half-brother Brett.

A minute later, she was at her usual spot in front of the fifth column from the stairs when she stifled a quick laugh as Rosalind tripped, sending her champagne flying in Dirk's direction. Full of mirth, her eyes rose from the page and there he was, in the same spot as last Thursday, calmly watching her. The slightest of smiles curled the corners of his lips and gave his eyes a distant twinkle. Without thinking, she smiled at him, a full, bright, happy-to-be-alive smile, but it faded when it was not returned. As happened the previous week, his eyes followed her to her seat before he entered the next car.

The following week he was in his spot before she arrived at hers. Her smile and nod were repaid with the same not-quite-a-smile he wore the previous week. It became a Thursday ritual.

By the middle of the third month, Sasha's curiosity got the better of her. Weirdo or not, she had to find out who he was and why he singled her out for attention. When the train arrived, she entered the car as usual, but instead of turning to take a seat, she continued forward toward the door on the other side. But at her first step beyond the point where she always turned, he turned and hurried to the next car. She followed. Though she entered soon after he did, he had already exited onto her platform and was entering her usual car.

She shrugged, took the hint, and a seat.

More weeks passed and she found herself wondering about him even on days that were not Thursday. Who was he? What did he do? Was he married? Was he someone's dad? Did he share her love of coffee? She wanted to know the answers to those questions and so many more, but he clearly did not want actual contact and she was not about to force herself on anyone. She continued to catch his eyes and almost always smiled at him as they waited for the train, but eventually, she stopped watching him as he watched her take her seat.

Today was their twenty-six week anniversary. It was the longest relationship she ever had with a guy she did not know. It was longer than most of her relationships with guys she did know.

At the bottom of the steps, it occurred to her that every Thursday for months now, she descended the stairs wondering if he would be there, as if there was a chance he would not be. He never missed a Thursday yet, so why did she wonder? For that matter, why did she care?

When she reached the platform and looked across the tracks, ready to smile, her stomach did a hollow flip. No Watcher.

But he must be here. He's always here!

She continued past her usual spot until she reached the end of the platform, but he really was not there.

Back at the fifth column, she tried to focus on the mystery of who killed the plumber who was really a jewel thief, but found concentration elusive.

Why do I feel unhappy about some weirdo not

showing up?

The question plagued her all day. Why should she care about some guy who was too shy or too *something* to do more than stare at her for six months?

So he didn't show this morning. So what? Maybe he got sick or he's on a vacation. Maybe he had an appointment somewhere. Maybe he just decided to stay home and watch daytime TV in his underwear. There's probably a zillion reasons. So why the hell am I making myself crazy over some weirdo?

The answer popped into her head.

Because he's my *weirdo! My god, that's it. I've started to think of The Watcher as my weirdo, like we have some, well, weird connection or something. He watches, I smile and read.*

She grunted.

I've actually been looking forward to Thursdays just so I can see him standing there across the tracks. God, how pathetic is that?

The question was still in her head after work as she waited for the train to take her home.

Enough already!

Sasha powered the Kindle and glued her eyes to the screen until the train made its appearance. She closed the leather cover and stationed herself three feet from the edge of the platform. When the doors opened, she settled in a seat next to a woman who looked a little like her grandmother and opened the cover again as someone took the seat next to her, on the other side of a chrome pole. When the train began to move, she grabbed the pole to steady herself so she wouldn't bump the lady.

With her other hand, she clicked for the next page. As it appeared, a male voice said, "May I ask what it is you're reading?"

She froze, not from fear, but from surprise. Unless a

train was stalled in a tunnel thanks to a breakdown or power outage, strangers simply did not speak to one another as they rode. She often wondered why, since it would make the journey so much more enjoyable than just staring at the floor or reading the advertising displayed above the windows, but that was the way it was when she moved to the city, as she learned from the silent scowl she received in reply to her "good morning" the first time she rode the system and she wasn't about to lead a crusade to change it.

"A murder mystery," she said. Her head turned toward the voice. Whatever she planned to say next was lost when she saw who spoke to her.

Ohmygod! It's him! What do I say? What do I do? Why is he here? Why...

His smile slammed the breaks on her racing thoughts. It was a great smile, full of warmth, and joy. "I expect you're a little confused, perhaps even apprehensive at finding me sitting next to you after six months?"

His deep, gold-flecked brown eyes held her hypnotized but she managed to nod.

"I'd very much like to explain, but it will take longer than the time to our stop. My name is Daniel Bower."

With a shake of her head, she recovered her voice and asked, "Why me?"

"I'm sorry?"

"Why me. Why did you pick me to stare at for six months?"

"Because you called to me. Not with your voice, of course. But when I saw you walk onto the platform that first day, I felt…something. I've tried to understand it for six months but I can't. Whatever it was, I knew you were someone special, someone very special I needed to meet. And why it had to take so long will have to wait. Here's our stop."

This is absolutely freaking crazy.

She walked beside him toward the exit.

But his eyes. The way they look into me. And his smile.

By the time they reached the street, she thought of a dozen reasons she should run and not look back. But she had to know, had to understand the past six months, why he watched, why he ran, why she thought of him so often and began to look forward to seeing him. There were so many questions and she wanted answers.

"I live…" He looked around, trying to get a bearing, then pointed off to the left. "…that way, I think. I always use the Kenton Street entrance, which is how I end up on the center platform. I'm sorry, but I don't know this area. Is there a place where we can sit and talk? Perhaps get coffee, or drinks, or dinner? Your choice."

She caught his eyes and held them, looking for a clue, a sign, anything that might settle the argument the logical side of her brain was having with the emotional one.

How can you know what he says is true?

Look at his eyes, they're kind and gentle.

So are those of an actor acting and a player on the prowl.

But he ran that time. He had me and ran. Why would he do that if he was just trying to game me?

When the logical side had no answer, she decided.

"Let's start with coffee and see where it goes from there."

She led him to a café a block from the entrance where they ordered at the counter before taking seats at a table in the back corner.

His eyes joined his mouth in a smile. At the question posed by her raised eyebrows, he said, "I've been anticipating this moment for months." When her brow furrowed, he added, "In the beginning, I was so wrapped up in what you'll hear about in a few minutes, it never occurred to me to wonder about you. I thought about you almost every day, but in terms of a person who somehow magically brought me peace at a time when I needed it more than anything else. That changed after a few weeks. I became curious about you, who you were, what you did, what you liked to read. But I've been most curious about one question, a personal question. May I ask it?"

Her mind raced with possibilities and then responses. She chose the safe one. "Yes you may, although whether or not I answer will depend on the nature of the question."

She could almost feel the warmth of his grin. "Fair enough. What is your first name?"

That one, obvious question had not been among the possibilities and caused her to laugh. "My name is Sasha."

"Ah! Such a beautiful name! Sasha. Thank you.

"You will need some background to fully understand the past six months, so I'll start at the beginning.

"I have always been somewhat conservative and, for the most part, was always attracted to conservative women. So when I met Diane, it was like a child of the desert tasting ice cream for the first time. I could not get enough of her. She was a free spirit looking for stability and I was desperate for someone unconventional who could draw me out. We clicked immediately and married eight months later. Ten months after that, Maria was born. She's six now.

"Although she loosened me up and I calmed her down, by our second anniversary it was clear she was unhappy. By our third, she was out of the house more nights than she was home, partying with old friends who were back in her life again, and new friends, many of them men. She spent Maria's third birthday in rehab and came home a week before her fourth from her second two-month stint.

"We had a nice ten months or so after that. I allowed myself to believe she truly changed and for nearly a year it seemed she had. Then I received a call on my cell one Wednesday morning. I was in Philadelphia on business for the week. It was Maria's school. She'd not been in school all week. They'd been trying to reach Diane at the house and on her cell since the day before but she never answered and never returned messages.

"I was on the next flight back and when I walked into the house, I found Diane and some guy naked on the living room floor with her legs wrapped around him as they…well. The room was littered with empty bottles, the coffee table looked like a pharmacy, and all I could think of was Maria. I must have shouted something because the guy looked up at me as he continued…you know…and asked Diane, 'Who the hell is that'? She answered, 'Nobody. Just my husband.' That's when I heard Maria calling 'daddy' from upstairs. She must have been screaming it. I found her in her room. She'd been locked in since Sunday night."

"Oh my god! Was she…"

"She was okay. Her room has a bathroom and Diane had filled a trash bag with all the junk food in the cabinets, but she was scared, mostly from the noises she heard from downstairs.

"As you may imagine, the police were familiar with our house, so I called them, explained the situation and that I'd left the front door open, and asked them to come, send the guy on his way, and then arrest Diane for child endangerment. When they arrived, the two were still going at it.

"Once they were gone I called Maria's school, called my sister to ask if Maria could stay with her until I could put the house back in order, then I phoned my attorney, who gave me the name of the best divorce lawyer in the city.

"The next morning, I was on my way to my first meeting with him. As you might imagine, I was more than a little depressed at the prospect of having to battle in court to retain custody of my daughter. The idea that she might be forced to live with Diane, to see…well, I was very depressed that day. Then you walked onto the platform and that's when whatever happened happened. I noticed you and felt…lighter. Not exactly happy, but hopeful. And each time you peeked over the reader to see if I was still looking at you I felt a little better.

"I thought about you all week and wondered, hoped, really, that I'd see you again the next week. And when I did, the same hopeful feeling returned. Then, when you laughed at something you were reading, all the dread I felt just went away. I know how bizarre it all sounds…" He shrugged. "…but it's the truth."

"Why did you run away the time I tried to meet you?" She watched his face fill with embarrassment.

"Yes. I'm sorry about that. It's not that I didn't…" He paused for a deep breath. "By that time, I was being followed full-time by someone hired by her lawyer. They were desperate to find something they could use against me. Gazing at someone on another subway platform certainly wouldn't do, but if we met and talked, who knows what they could have done with that. I was afraid. I couldn't do anything that would put Maria at risk."

"But you could have just brushed me off."

His blush had faded somewhat, but returned with a vengeance. "No. I couldn't. By then, I'd started to feel something for you. A crush of sorts, perhaps. I'm not sure. You'd done so much for me without even knowing it, I just knew that if we did meet, there'd be no way I could hide it. And if they ever got that on film, it would seriously jeopardize things in court.

"Two days ago, the divorce was finalized."

"So fast?"

"I am…not without means, and have friends who have friends and lots of grease was applied to the system. She's barred from any contact beyond a weekly telephone call until she demonstrates to the court she's been drug and alcohol free for two years."

"Wow!"

"I know. It was way more than I ever expected. The judge was an older woman and I think she'd seen a few too many cases like this. And God bless her, when Maria talked to the judge in chambers and told her how scared she was being locked in her room, I swear the judge struggled to hold back tears. All I know is that she was one angry judge when she read her decision.

"That's the whole story except for a little confession. I sort of stalked you yesterday. I disguised myself and followed you to work, then came back in the afternoon so I'd know when you got out. It was the only way I could learn what train you'd be on coming home tonight."

"Well, I wouldn't exactly call that stalking. As for the rest of it, I don't know what to say. I mean, it's all so incredible."

"I know. I said I'd been looking forward to today, and it was for a few reasons. First, I wanted to thank you for just being who you are and where you were each Thursday. Just knowing I'd see you every Thursday, thinking about your smile and your laugh, kept me going from week to week. No matter what happens from this moment on, I will never forget you and I will always be grateful."

He noticed the rosy glow that came to her cheeks and thought it made her look even lovelier. "Now for the part I've been dreading. Are you married or engaged or otherwise in a committed relationship?"

Her short laugh took him by surprise. "I'm sorry," she said. "I wasn't laughing at you. Your question just reminded me of something I was thinking about this morning. But the answer is no, Daniel, I'm not involved with anyone."

His joy at hearing her answer was unmistakable. "I'm happy to hear that. I…" His phone began to ring. "I'm sorry. I forgot to put it on silent. Let me…oh!" He looked up at her. "It's Maria."

"Go. Talk."

"Hi, sweetie. … Yes, I'm done working. … No, I'm talking with a friend." He rolled his eyes. "Her name is Sasha. … I do, too. Now… If Aunt Sue said no then no it is. Now blow me a kiss and say good bye. I'll see you a little later. … I love you, too. Bye sweetie."

He grinned and shrugged his eyebrows. "Sorry. She's curious as the proverbial cat. I told her I'd be late tonight because I was meeting someone but didn't have a name to give her. I figured she'd find some way to get Susan to let her call."

"She sounds precocious and adorable. Do you have a picture?"

"I do, but I can't let you see it. She is *so* beautiful, if I show you the picture, you'll fall in love with *her* and where would that leave me?"

"Right about where you are now?"

"Exactly.

"Sasha, that first morning, I'd been standing there for quite awhile, paralyzed by what happened and by the thought of what could happen. Two trains came and went and many women walked into my line of stare. But it was you, or something about you, that reached into me and brought me back to life.

"I've pretty much convinced myself it was fate or a

guardian angel that kept me glued to the platform until you arrived. And if all this hasn't convinced you that I'm some kind of lunatic, I would very much like to get to know you and to let you get to know me. Maybe we're destined to be friends or maybe something more. Maybe we're just two trains passing on their separate journeys. But whatever it is, I want us to have the chance to find out."

Daniel walked home slowly, replaying everything from the moment he first spoke to her on the train. The anxious part of him wished he stayed longer and did more to convince her, but the rational part knew he did all he could. Despite her smile, despite the quick hug as they parted, he could see how conflicted she was. All he could do now is hope that somehow she felt the truth of it, that she could accept what he knew she saw in his eyes.

Forty-five minutes later, he was sitting in Sulmona Pizza listening to Maria recount her day in school when his phone rang.

"Did you leave your homework at Aunt Sue's house again?" he asked before flipping the phone open and saying, "Hello."

"I have one condition and it's non-negotiable."

"And that is?"

"If we make it past the second date, I get to see the picture."

The Highway Man

Sandy stood at the railing, checking out the prospects in the large backyard. She nodded toward the left side of the patio.

"There's a cute one," she said to Lisa, who was similarly occupied.

"And the one he's talking to is pretty hot, too."

"True, but he's not my flavor. You're welcome to him if you can get him."

"If? Get real, girl. What man is going to say no to this?" She shook her blond mane and took a step back, her hands splayed out to her sides. "I have the look, I have the attitude, and I *know* how to use them!"

She laughed and Sandy joined her.

"When are you going to get over this flavor thing?" Lisa asked. "Chocolate, mocha, coffee, butter pecan, vanilla, they're all the same. Guys want food and drink and sex. And lots of them will settle for just sex, especially the ones with money."

"I'm not just looking to get laid, Lisa. You know that."

"Why the hell not? You're twenty-three and got it going and there's lots of time for picket fences. Have some fun."

"I had plenty of fun in college, with every shape and size the good Lord created and you know what? Big or small, not a one did me any better than I could do myself. 'Cause it was just sex.

"Hey, Carol," she said as their hostess walked by. "Who's the cute guy in the tan shirt over there?"

"Steve something. He's Barry's friend from work."

"Another engineer?"

Carol shrugged.

Lisa nudged her. "What about the guy he's talking to?"

"I'm not sure. But from that look on your face, I think he's going to be very happy tonight. Come on. I'll introduce you to Steve. He probably knows Mr. Lucky's name."

As the women approached, they saw two sets of eyes send serious appreciation their way.

"Steve, these are my friends, Sandy and Lisa. Ladies, Steve."

"Please to meet you," he said. "This is Bill."

"Good afternoon," Bill said as Carol waved and left to greet other guests. His eyes locked on Sandy. "You look lovely. The green matches your eyes."

"Thank you for noticing."

After a few seconds, he realized he was staring and turned to Lisa. "And you look smashing." He chuckled. "I've wanted to say that to a woman ever since I heard some British guy say it in a movie."

As the four talked, it became clear to both guys the women had called dibs in advance. Steve was happy. He was more than a little partial to nicely packaged brunettes. Bill was similarly partial, but he was happy to spend an afternoon with an exuberant blonde.

The evening sun cast long shadows when Sandy

found Lisa on the front porch. "Where's Bill?"

"He left awhile ago. Said he had to go to work."

"On a Saturday night? What does he do?"

"I didn't ask. But it can't be much. I mean, he was wearing off-the-rack clothes from Sears or something."

"Lisa, you are such a snob."

"Hey, I like men of means. Still, when he said he had to leave soon, I tried to get him into the bathroom for a quickie."

"God, Lisa."

"God, Lisa what? His clothes might have been nothing special, but he filled out certain parts pretty well. And it's been four days. Besides, I think he liked you better. I noticed him looking your way a few times. I would have sent him over to you if he wasn't the wrong flavor. What happened with Steve?"

"Nothing. He was nice enough but he was just looking to get laid."

"Damn! Why the hell didn't you send him to me? I'd have gladly traded for Bill. And I wouldn't even have cared what he was packing."

An hour later, Sandy dropped off Lisa and pulled onto the highway for the drive home. As the lights of the city faded in her rear view mirror, she wondered what kind of man would have turned down a quickie with Lisa, especially the way she was dressed.

Maybe I should *have sent Steve over to her after the fourth time he hinted. They clearly would have been perfect for each other and Lisa would be calling me tomorrow thanking me. Oh well.*

She was about ten miles from home when the car's engine made a funny sound, the car jerked, and died. She had the presence of mind to immediately shift into neutral and test the brakes. She had to push hard, but they worked. She coasted into the breakdown lane and stopped close to the guard rail.

"Great. Just what I need at this hour."

With her road-club card in hand she called and gave her approximate location.

"A truck from Hodge Brothers should be there within thirty minutes. If possible, for safety, we recommend you wait at the side of the road, not in the vehicle."

Sandy popped the trunk, grabbed her bag, and said a prayer of thanks for the warm night and full moon. It wasn't that she was afraid of the dark, she was just concerned about animals that prowled after dark. She took the thick, woolen blanket from her trunk, laid it across the guard rail, and sat down to wait.

She began counting the cars and trucks that went by, but tired of that after a few minutes. Then she picked out what few constellations she could recognize despite the bright moonlight. Memories of her last relationship filled the next few minutes and were followed by a slightly off-key rendition of *If This Was A Movie*. She just finished the second chorus when a car whizzed by in the first lane then braked and pulled into the breakdown lane a few hundred feet ahead. The car backed up until it was about twenty feet from hers.

"Car trouble, huh?" the man said, his voice scratchy from too many years of smoking cigarettes like the one hanging from his lips.

"Yes. It just stopped. I called the auto club. They should be here soon."

"Maybe you want some company while you wait."

"No thanks, I'm fine. They'll be here in a few minutes."

"What's the matter? You don't like me or something?"

Oh shit. What do I do now?

"It's not that. I just have a lot to think about for work next week."

He took a long drag on the cigarette then dropped it and ground it out with his shoe. "Can't be starting no forest fires now, can we?" He was at the front of the car, just a few feet from her when he detoured to the driver's side and looked in the windows.

"You been out shopping or something?"

"No, just coming home from a small party at a friend's house."

Just keep him talking until the truck gets here.

"Is that right." He continued around the car until he was standing next to her. "You know, it's dangerous for girls to be out alone at night. All kinds of things can happen. Wild animals could come out of the woods there and bite them or even kill them and drag them off to eat them. Or a bad man could stop and force her to do things she might not like."

Sandy was shaking now, so scared she couldn't have cried if she tried.

He'd probably like it if I cried. He'd probably get off on it. Please God, get me out of this. Why did I let him get so close? How fucking stupid am I? What...

"Or maybe he'd just cut her throat and steal whatever she had in her bag and in her trunk."

She heard a sharp click and knew it was the sound of a switchblade opening.

"Of course, if the girl took out her wallet and gave it to the bad man as a gift, because she liked him, and then gave him her keys, maybe the bad man wouldn't cut her throat. Maybe he'd just thank her for the gifts and leave."

She was trembling so hard her voice quaked as she said, "I'd appreciate it if you would accept my wallet and anything you find in my car or trunk that you want as gifts for staying with me and protecting me. The keys are in the ignition and the wallet's in my bag. Would you like to get it or would you like me to take it out?"

"Well, now, that's really nice of you to make an offer like that. I accept. I'll be happy to get it so as not to trouble you."

She held out her bag and he took it.

"You ain't got no mousetrap or nothing in here, do you?"

The question was so absurd under the circumstances, a quickly stifled laugh burst from her.

"See how much fun we're having. Laughing and giving presents."

He shifted the bag to his other hand and she could see the blade of the knife she heard open. He grabbed her wallet and shoved it in his pocket.

"What else you got in here? Anything good?" His hand closed around a plastic cylinder. "What's this, a vibrator for when you're lonely?" He laughed at his own joke. "Oh. A flashlight. Now that's smart, carrying a flashlight for when you get stuck in the dark."

He flicked the switch and aimed it at her face, then went silent for almost fifteen seconds.

"Whoa! You're a looker." The light moved from her face down to her feet and back up again. "Oh yeah. You're a real beauty.

"Stand up and don't even think about running 'cause if you do, this knife will be sticking out of your back before you even take ten steps."

She stood and faced him as he tossed her bag on the hood. He played the light up and down again, then told her to turn around and repeated the motion. Cars and trucks continued to whoosh past every five to ten seconds.

She fought down the urge to scream.

Doesn't anyone see what's happening here? Are they all blind?

At his order, she turned to face him again. He slowly backed up and told her to walk forward until she was even with the front passenger door.

"Unbutton your shirt."

She hesitated, wondering if dying with a knife in her back would be preferable to being raped by this animal.

"I said unbutton your shirt if you want to get home in one piece tonight."

She reached for the top button just as a vehicle pulled into the breakdown lane about a quarter-mile ahead and began to brake.

"What the fuck," the man said as the headlights slowly illuminated them. "Fuckin' auto club." With a few quick steps he was standing behind her.

The point of the knife touched her back and she stiffened. "Relax. That was just a reminder it was there. When he gets here, you tell him everything's okay. Tell him I'm your boyfriend. Bob. And that I fixed it. If you fuck it up, I'll kill him and do you up so bad you'll be begging me to kill you. Understand?"

She nodded.

He kneed her behind. "Do you understand?"

"Yes, I understand. You're my boyfriend, the car is fixed, and he can just go."

"Very good. I think you and I are gonna have some fun later, and I think you're gonna live to remember it. If you're smart and do exactly as you're told."

The driver put the truck in PARK, took a phone from his pocket, and pressed the CONNECT button. "Gloria, I'm at the dead car."

"Okay, boss."

He looked at the scene and felt something was not right.

"Gloria, who called this one in?"

"The club said the member, Sandy Gilman. Said she

was waiting with the car."

"Okay, thanks."

Two cars. A guy standing behind the woman. Neither one looks happy to see me. Odd.

He grabbed his clipboard.

Sandy watched the driver climb out of the truck and approach them, his features lost in the glare of the headlights. She wasn't sure if the fear left her, if it became so intense her brain turned it off to protect itself, or if she somehow accepted she might die there tonight on the side of the highway. All she knew was that she felt calm and her thoughts were as sharp as the knife at her back. One wrong word and she knew he'd stab her. Yet somehow, she had to let the driver know she needed help. There was only one way she could think of and she had to do it before the driver said anything.

As he reached the back of her car, he looked up from his clipboard.

Hey, isn't that...what the hell?

She was mouthing the word 'help' over and over.

He removed his cap and reset it on his head, pulling the bill low over his eyes. "Hi, folks. Are you Sandy Gilman?"

"Yes. This is my boyfriend, Bob. He came along a little while ago and fixed the car so we won't be needing a tow or anything. I'm sorry you had to drive all the way out here for nothing."

"Oh, that's no problem, ma'am. The report says the car made a noise and then just went dead. Is that right?"

"Yes."

"I'm kind of new at this job. A few weeks, you know? Would you mind telling me what it was, Bob, so I'll know for the next time?"

"A wire came off. I just finished putting it back on when you showed up."

"That would be the wire from the distribution manifold?"

"Yeah, that one."

"Okay, good. I had one like that the beginning of last week. Anyway, I just need to verify the car starts and I can go back and catch the end of the game."

"You don't need to do that," Bob said.

"Geez, I do. I already got in trouble once for not verifying and the guy's car got about a quarter-mile down the road and the whole engine seized. These new computer controlled cars are so damn tricky, half the time I have to call the boss at the station just to find out what button to push." As he talked, he walked to the driver's side of the car. He opened the door and said, "I'll just be a second."

He heard Bob yell, "Hey," but he was already in the car and turning the key. Nothing happened.

"I knew it," he said as got out and reached down to release the hood latch. "When you reset the rebostadt, you forgot to press in both buttons at the same time."

"The what?" Bob said.

"The rebostadt. The little box on the side of the manifold. You forgot to reset them, didn't you. Well don't feel bad. I forgot last week, too. And I bet you forgot to check the framersholm to make sure *it* didn't pop? That's okay, it shouldn't take more than fifteen or twenty minutes to reset everything, unless the framersholm did pop. That'll take a little longer, but I know I have one in the truck if we need it."

He kept his head down as he walked to the front of the car, noting how the guy moved himself and the girl halfway toward the back.

"Look, buddy, we don't have time to wait. We got to get somewhere. Just tow the thing to your garage and we'll pick it up tomorrow or Monday."

"Are you sure?"

"Yes. Right, honey?"

"Yes. Yes. Just tow it."

"Okay then, I just need to make a tow order and get your signature." He put his clipboard on the hood and walked back to the truck. Then he turned and yelled, "You want it to go to the shop, right?" and watched both of them nod. "Okay, I just have to call and let them know."

Once in the cab, he took the phone from his pocket and pressed CONNECT. "Gloria. Call the state police now. Tell them it's an emergency. A woman's being held hostage. Give them my GPS coordinates and tell them to come in without lights just in case. And tell them to hurry."

Outside, Bob leaned close to Sandy's ear and said, "You're doing real good, sweetheart. Real good. I'm gonna make sure you enjoy yourself later for being so good."

She felt her stomach churn at the thought of what he might do to her but steeled herself, refusing to vomit in disgust.

The driver slid a tow form from the pack and stepped down from the truck. He walked straight to the front of the car, slid the form under the clip, and began to fill it out using the information on the service call printout.

"Gilman with one L, right?"

"Yes."

"27 Broadhurst Ave. in Hudson?"

"Yes."

"Great. I just need you to sign this and you folks can be on your way."

As he came around the car, he grabbed her bag from the hood.

"Here you go, ma'am," he said, holding it out. "Oh,

wait, you can't sign while you're holding a bag."

He thrust it at Bob. As Bob's hand closed on the bag, the driver extended the clipboard toward Sandy as he took a step away from them both, then put all his weight and muscle into a vicious shoulder check that caught Bob square on the sternum and sent him flying back over the guard rail.

"Run to the truck," he yelled. "Get in and lock the doors. Don't open them for anyone but me or the cops."

His head flipped back and forth, watching her get into the truck while watching for Bob to get back on his feet. Just as Sandy closed the door, Bob stepped over the guardrail.

"You're gonna die for that, tow man. You're gonna die real slow and then she's gonna die even slower."

He expected his victim to show fear at the sight of the blade, but the guy just stood there, smiling.

"You know, Bob, I grew up around guys like you. Tough guys, who liked to show women who was boss, who got off on hearing them beg and cry. I got out of there as soon as I could. Joined the army, saw the world, and in between, learned how to turn guys like you into a mass of broken bones and jelly.

"The way you hold that blade makes me think you know how to use it. That's good. It'll almost make it a fair fight. Almost, but not quite. Personally, I think your best bet is to throw it and hope I don't catch it and throw it back and accidentally sever your dick. Or you might want to just toss it on the ground over there and then lay yourself on the ground with your fingers laced behind your head."

Bob stared for a second in disbelief, then growled and said, "Fuck you, asshole" as he moved in for the kill.

What happened next happened so fast, Sandy, who watched from the safety of the truck, wasn't quite sure exactly what *did* happen. One second, the two were facing each other, then Bob moved toward the driver, and then Bob was on the ground with a shattered knee, one broken arm, the other dislocated, and testicles that felt like they had shot up into his throat before snapping back.

She watched as the driver put a foot on Bob's neck.

"I tried to warn you, guy. Don't worry about lacing your fingers behind your head."

He removed the phone from his pocket. "Gloria, call the police again. Tell them the situation has been resolved, so they can come in with lights. And tell them we'll need an ambulance."

He turned his head toward the truck and waved for Sandy to come out. When she was a few feet away, he removed his hat.

"You! From the party! Bill!"

"William Hodge at your service. I cannot believe how calm you were. Did he have that shiv at your back the whole time?"

She nodded.

"Lord, you are one tough woman. Mouthing 'help' right at the start was inspired."

"How did you do that to him? I saw it, but all I remember is a blur."

"That means I did it right."

Blue lights, followed by red ones, appeared over the hill.

"Cops are coming. Trash pickup, too.

"When they get here, do your best to tell them everything you can remember, every detail, everything he said. The more you can give them, the easier it will be to lock him up for a very long time."

"Fuck you, asshole," drifted up from the ground. "I just stopped to help the lady and you attacked me. I'm gonna own your ass and everything else you have."

Bill looked at Sandy who just smiled and shook her head. Then she leaned close to his ear and whispered, "He still has my wallet in his pocket."

Ninety minutes later Bill pulled the flatbed into the yard of Hodge Motors. "I sure am glad I got this call," he told Sandy, who was sitting next to him in the truck. "Not only did I get to beat up a scumbag and save a beautiful woman, I got two, count 'em, two tows in one trip and one of them is probably going to sit in storage for awhile at twenty bucks a day until the cops get around to it, if they ever do." He laughed. "Best run I've had in a long time. Come on in the office. I have to do some quick paperwork and then I'll drive you home."

Sandy watched as he typed, printed, and signed half-a-dozen forms, then handed her one. "That's for your car. I'll get the new timing belt and install it Monday. Then I'll drive it to you and have one of the guys follow me to take me back here."

"Bill, you don't have to do all that."

"Oh but I do. It's a service we offer to every woman who's nearly kidnapped by a maniac." He grinned and wiggled his eyebrows, which made her laugh.

"Can I ask you something?"

"Sure."

"If I hadn't been able to mouth 'help'…"

"It wouldn't have mattered. I suspected something was wrong when I arrived. Guys don't stand behind women like that unless they're getting their picture taken. And as soon as he agreed he plugged in the wire to the distribution manifold, I was pretty sure he was lying. It's a distributor cap. And the wires don't just pop out for no reason. But then I threw the rebostadt and framersholm at him and when he didn't call me on them I was sure. They're made-up words. And honestly, even if I had doubts after that, just watching you two would have been enough."

Sandy sat quietly for a minute, nodding, thinking about what he said and what he had done.

"Bill, I…I don't know how it's possible to thank you for what you did tonight. I owe you my life. But even if he didn't end up killing me, I can't imagine living with the memory of what he would have done to me." Her whole body shuddered at the thought. Then it stopped, her eyes closed, and he saw her cringe, as if in pain.

"Are you okay?"

"Yes. No. I don't know. Can I ask you another question?"

He nodded.

"Lisa told me what she did at the party and that you turned her down. Why?"

"Because that's not me. That kind of sex, it's like using someone else's body to masturbate." He held up a hand. "I don't need someone else for that. Why do you ask?"

"Because I thought all guys like any kind of sex they can get."

"Some do, some don't. Many do when they're young but outgrow it."

"I guess. Like some girls." She studied him for a few seconds. "At the party, when we met, despite how Lisa was dressed, you caught my eye first and complimented me. And Lisa said she noticed you looking at me a few times during the party. Why?"

"Because when I met you, I was struck by the way you looked. And I just naturally prefer brunettes to blondes. But it was more than that. I felt something about you was different from any other woman I'd ever met. I didn't know what it was, but I'd have liked to find out. I guess tonight we discovered what at least part of it was."

"And it didn't bother you that we were different?"

"Well, no. I like that girls and boys are different."

"That's not what I meant."

"I know. You meant different flavors."

Sandy's eyes widened. "Lisa…"

"Yes. She told me when she realized how interested I was. I guess she thought she was doing me a favor so I wouldn't waste my time."

Sandy dropped her eyes. "When you asked me if I was okay before, it was because I was ashamed of feeling that way. And you knew it and still you risked your life to save me."

"Yeah, guys sometimes do pretty dumb things for women they're attracted to."

"If I ask you, will you come home and stay with me tonight?"

"No. I don't sleep with women I don't know. But I'd love to take you out for brunch tomorrow."

Sandy smiled. "I'd like that."

Exhaustion chose that moment to assert itself. "Will you take me home, now? I need a long, hot shower and sleep."

They stood and as he reached for the doorknob her hand intercepted his. Holding it, she said, "I can't leave without thanking you properly." Then she kissed him and his arms slid around her and pulled her close as he kissed her back. And when their lips finally parted, hers smiled and said, "Mmmmm. I think this flavor might grow on me."

The Duck Pond

Charlotte pulled into the parking lot, shut off the engine, set the brake, and released the tears she held back for the twelve minutes it took to drive to the Duck Pond.

The spot was not a real pond. It was the place where the river tripped over a dam in a pretty little waterfall and expanded some as it made a wide left turn on its way to the lake a bit over a mile away. It was the place her father took her and her brother most Sunday mornings when they were young.

It changed some since then, as various town administrations tried to improve on nature's raw beauty, but it was still the one place Charlotte knew she could always come to find peace. And if she brought a loaf of bread, as her father did all those quiet, wonderful Sundays, she could even feed the ducks.

She had no bread today, though. Only a heart full of pain, a soul darkened with despair, and eyes overflowing with tears. She sat and wept and cursed the day they met, him with his toothy grin, the thought of which even now, as she sat there hating him, caused her to melt a little inside. She shook her head and banished the image. There would be no forgiving this time.

She crossed her hands on top of the steering wheel

before her head fell forward to rest on them. Sobs shook her body as she gave up her attempt at control and released all the emotion built up over three wasted years of her life.

Long, bitter minutes later, a knock on her window caused her to start. She turned her head enough to see a small boy, maybe five or six years old, standing next to her car with a worried look on his face. She shook her head and waved him away and watched as he turned and ran toward the pond. Then she leaned back and closed her eyes, but the tears continued to force themselves between the lids and roll down her now blotchy cheeks.

Another knock interrupted her misery. The boy had returned and brought a man who was making circles in the air with his finger. She caught herself and sighed and rolled the window down a few inches.

"I'm very sorry," the man said. "Nicky told me there was a lady in a car who was hurt. He associates tears with being hurt."

She looked at the boy. "I'm not hurt, Nicky, but thank you for being concerned."

The man handed Nicky a half-full bag of bread and said, "Why don't you go back and feed the ducks some more. But stay on the walk. And remember to break the slices into little pieces so they don't choke."

He watched the child until he reached the walkway and looked back, then turned to Charlotte and said, "Please forgive me, but I can tell that whatever caused you to look like this is pretty serious. Is there anything we can do to help?"

The corners of her lips curled at the thought of a little boy confronting the asshole. Then she shook her head. "No. Thank you. I'll…I'll be fine."

"What's his name?"

The inquiry startled her. She looked up at him and

could see in his eyes that he knew. But how could he? She watched a sadness come over him.

"I've seen that look more times than I care to remember. Deaths, illness, accidents, they're all different. But only some world-class jerk can make a woman look the way you do right now."

He saw the questions in her eyes, smiled, and reached into his pocket for his identification. "I'm a cop here in town. Detective, actually. If you like, I could go arrest the S.O.B. for being a disgrace to his gender. Put the handcuffs on real tight. Maybe bump his head as I put him in the back of the patrol car? What do you think?"

Despite everything, a smile and laugh broke through. "I'm not sure lying and cheating are felonies yet, but thank you for offering."

"Why don't you come feed the ducks with us. Or walk around for a while. I've been coming here since I was younger than Nicky and feeding the ducks or just sitting on the grass looking out at the water has never failed to cheer me up when I was down."

An hour later, they were parked on the grass while Nicky rolled down the gentle slope, jumped up with a laugh, then raced to the top for another roll.

"I wish I still felt that free, that uninhibited," she said.

"I know what you mean. Go ahead. Give it a whirl. Nicky will love it."

"No," she said, her head unconsciously shaking, "I couldn't. That's not me anymore."

"It's funny how adulthood gives us so many new freedoms, but at the price of so many of the ones that made life a blast when we were kids. I used to do that here, almost in the same spot, when I was his age."

"Me, too. My dad used to take us here every Sunday morning."

"No kidding! Do you mind if I ask how old you are?"

"Twenty-seven."

"I'll be…oh god…I'll be thirty in two months. But my mom and dad used to bring me here all the time. There used to be a pergola built on top of a brick and concrete platform and we'd have picnics there."

"Yes! I remember that. And I remember being sad when I showed up one day and it was gone. Just the platform remained. And then…maybe a year or so later, that was gone too, replaced with more grass."

"I wonder if we were ever here at the same time? Probably so. Though I'm ashamed to admit I'd never have paid you any attention. I was somewhat of a mini-misogynist as a boy."

"That's okay. Until puberty hit, I was firmly of the opinion that all boys except my father were basically booger-brains."

They shared a laugh before he said, "You look much better now than you did in the car."

"I feel much better, too. I appreciate you getting me out here. But I'm curious about something. You never told me your name or asked me mine. Why?"

"Well, I told you I've seen a lot of women in the state you were in a while ago. There are a lot of guys who would take advantage of that vulnerability. I didn't want you to think I was, you know, coming on to you or anything. I just wanted you to be able to hang out with Nicky and me or walk around or whatever without worrying about anything."

"So! You're an officer *and* a gentleman."

He chuckled at the word-play, but seemed embarrassed as he shrugged and said, "I try my best at both."

"Then your wife or girlfriend is a very lucky woman."

"Thank you. I agree. Or would if I had one of either at the moment."

They shared another laugh.

"Well, Charles Fitzgerald, my name is Charlotte Clarkson and I…"

"Wait! How did you know…" She watched his brow furrow as he ran time backwards in his head. Then he smiled. "My ID. How in the world did you read it though all those tears?"

It was her turn to shrug. "I don't know. But it was the only thing I noticed on it. And now I think it's time to go tell Robert I've had quite enough of him and his smile and his lies and throw his sorry ass out of my condo for good."

Charles reached into his pocket again, withdrew a card, and handed it to her. "My cell is on the back. If he gives you any trouble, and Charlotte, I mean any trouble at all, please call me. You won't be imposing and you won't be disturbing me, even if it's three in the morning. Do not get into an argument with him. I've seen too many of these things escalate and…well, I don't want you to get hurt."

He stood and held out a hand to help her to her feet.

"Thank you again for everything, Charles. You've almost restored my faith in men."

"Only almost?"

"Hey, it's a start. Did you say you bring Nicky here every Saturday morning?"

"Unless it's raining."

"Then perhaps I'll see you again sometime. And I promise to call if there's any trouble at all."

She began to leave but stopped and looked back over her shoulder. "You're a good man, Charles Fitzgerald. The world needs more like you."

~ ~ ~

The week went by much too slowly for Charles. By the time he picked up Nicky, he was having regular, very unprofessional thoughts about seeing Charlotte again. As he and Nicky fed ducks, ran around, and had fun, he kept one eye on the parking lot, watching for a particular green Toyota. And later, as he drove his nephew home, he realized he felt a real sense of loss that it never arrived, though he wasn't quite sure how he could lose something he never had. Still, he remained hopeful.

When she did not come after the second week, he drove to work the next day with the intention of finding out where she lived and, perhaps, give her a call to see how she was doing. But he never ran the search. He did not want to become one of the guys who chase after the newly single, the hurt and vulnerable. Nobody knows better than a cop that life does not always work out the way you hope it will. Three weeks later, he only wondered about her once or twice a day.

~ ~ ~

It was a beautiful Saturday and the morning sun warmed Charles and Nicky as they wrestled on the grass. He had just let Nicky pin him for the third time when he stood, turned, and felt his heart stop. There she was, walking toward them, smiling.

"I'm happy to hear there was no trouble," he said a few minutes later as they sat on the grass watching Nicky throw bits of bread into the water. "Ever since that day, I've wondered what happened. I thought you might come the following Saturday."

"No, I was kind of a mess for a couple of weeks. I didn't want you to see me like that, even though you'd seen me much worse that day. I couldn't understand why, as much as I hated him for all the cheating and the lies, as happy as I was to see the door close behind him, my heart still ached. But you helped me get over that."

"Me? How?"

"I began comparing how Robert treated me to how you treated me, and every time I did that, he faded a little more until the ache was gone. Then I started wondering how you were doing, if you'd caught many bad guys, if you'd found that wife or girlfriend yet?"

He laughed. "It's only been five or six weeks! But to tell the truth, I've thought about you, too."

"Is that so?"

"It is. I…enjoyed talking with you that day once you regained your composure. It was easy to see you were smart and funny and I found myself wishing I'd met you under different circumstances."

"What kind of circumstances?"

"A party, a club, in the supermarket. Anywhere we would have just been a man and a woman with the chance to get to know one another."

Warmth replaced the anxiety she had been feeling. "And what is it that we are right here, right now?"

He hesitated only second before venturing, "A man and a woman with the chance to get to know one another?"

"There you go. But there are two things I have to know before I can even think of going out with you."

"And they are?"

"First…" She leaned over and gave him a soft kiss. "Nice. Promising."

"And the second thing?"

She jumped up and pulled him to his feet. "Will you roll down the hill with me?"

Moving On

Paula wrapped her legs around him and dug her heels into his butt cheeks, lifting herself to meet his thrusts. "Faster," she whispered as her eyes closed and she pretended it was *him* inside her. "Faster."

He picked up the pace as her fantasy replayed. Their meeting in the grocery store, the way his tall, lean frame, wild, sandy hair, and mischievous smile from across the produce bin made her knees weak, her heart flutter, and her panties itch. His sweet words, the fire in his eyes, all for her. Locking the bathroom door, ripping her panties from beneath her skirt, lifting her, pressing her back against the cold tile wall as he plunged deep inside, touching her spot over and over.

"Yes, yes, just like that. Deeper, harder."

Her muscles contracted around him in rhythm with each thrust, heightening the pleasure, bringing her closer and closer. Deep, unconscious grunts penetrated her fantasy.

No! Not yet. I'm so close. I'm...

He buried himself to the hilt and she felt him throb over and over as he emptied his seed into the condom. Then he collapsed on her, spent.

Fuck!

She rolled him off, ignoring his attempt to hold her as she rose and shuffled to the bathroom. The harsh fluorescent light hurt her eyes as she stared into the mirror, trying to reconcile what she saw with what her mind remembered, and began to cry.

~ ~ ~

Camille strolled through the door and plopped onto the padded oak chair. "Do you have the paperwork ready for the Gravers deal? And good morning."

Paula shook her head. "Not yet. Still waiting for the inspection report. It's supposed to be faxed by ten. And good morning."

Camille took in the puffy eyes that makeup could not quite hide, the quickly brushed hair, the slumping shoulders and suppressed a sigh.

"Bad night last night?" she asked her partner and best friend.

Paula looked away as she shrugged.

"Oh, sweetie. Not again?"

"Please, Cam. Don't."

This time, the sigh escaped. She jumped up and closed the office door, then held up a hand when she saw anger flash across Paula's face.

"Paula, I love you as much as I love my sister, maybe more. And I've held my tongue for almost a year now while you scared me to death with all the booze and men. It's not your fault he died. It's just not."

A hand clutched her heart as tears began to drip from Paula's cheeks. It almost made her stop, but she knew she could not inflict any pain that her alter ego had not heaped upon herself for far too long.

"Kenny had a bad blood vessel in his brain. He didn't know. His doctor didn't know. It could have burst anytime, anywhere. That it happened while you were together was pure chance. An act of God. There was nothing you or anyone could have done to predict it or to stop it. It was just his time."

Tears continued to rain on Paula's blouse, her face a hard mask as Camille pulled the chair to the edge of the desk before sitting.

"I'm sorry, sweetie, I really am, but I'm so effing scared for you I can't sleep sometimes for worrying. Please. Please help me to understand why you do it. That's all. Just help me understand what the drinking and the one-night stands do for you. How they help you. You've been my best friend for my whole life and I thought we knew each other as well as we know ourselves. But I could never, *ever* have even imagined you this way. I know it hurts you to talk about it, but please, just this once, just you and me. Help me make sense of what you're doing."

She realized her own tears were falling now, as they sat in silence.

How many times have we cried together over the years? Must be hundreds.

Long minutes later, she thought something about Paula changed. She blinked, then swiped at her flooded eyes with her hands and was sure. She saw resignation in her eyes.

"The doctors, you, everyone. You're all wrong. It *was* my fault. *I* killed him. That sweet, gentle man with such a wild, wonderful side is dead because of me, because I was selfish."

"But you…"

"Stop. You wanted to hear it, so listen.

"Kenny was tired that night when he got home. But I'd been thinking about him all day, fantasizing about how we met, what we did, how I felt, everything, and I was so hot for him I could hardly keep from squirming on the chair as we ate supper. Then his brother called and Mike called and it was forever before he was off the phone. I could see in his eyes how tired he was but I was crazed by then. I wanted him, I needed him, and by god, I was gonna have him."

She sighed, pulled tissues from the box on her desk, and dabbed at her eyes and cheeks.

"I started playing him right there in the kitchen, getting him hot, getting him hard, you know? Then I started stripping and as soon as my panties hit the floor he reached for me and I jumped up and wrapped my legs around him so he could carry me to the bedroom. If he'd been naked, too, I'd have put him inside me but I had to wait for him to undress, which didn't take long.

"My whole body was on fire. We didn't even mess around first. I just lay on my back and he plunged in so hard and so deep I almost came. I think he sensed that because he didn't move even when I begged him to fuck me. He just waited and waited like that, throbbing inside me but never moving. Then he did. But I wasn't close anymore.

"He started pumping faster and kept hitting my spot deep inside and I went crazy with the feeling. But I wasn't getting close to coming again, so I told him to go faster and faster and wrapped my legs around him and heaved up to meet each thrust, begging him to do it harder and faster and then I felt it start and I started squeezing him and that brought me closer and closer but then he grunted and stopped and I screamed for him to finish me and then he collapsed on me. I was still so sex-crazed I kept pushing at him wiggling my hips and squeezing him, begging to come but it was already too late. Finally I realized he wasn't breathing and I screamed and rolled him off me and he was dead. Dead because I was too selfish to let him rest when he needed it. So selfish I kept pushing him harder and harder until it killed him."

Her whole body seemed to deflate at once as tears again spilled freely.

"Oh god, Paula, why didn't you ever tell me about this?"

She hurried around the desk, pulled her friend to her feet, and hugged her as she wept.

"You see," Paula whispered through her tears, "Now you know the truth. I was selfish and weak and I killed him. But I can't live without him. I love him so much and he's gone and every time I close my eyes I see him on top of me in the bed, not moving, not breathing, because of me. So I drink to forget what I did, what kind of person I am. But then I miss him, I miss him so much it hurts. I miss him holding me, and kissing me. I miss him inside of me. So I go with someone. And for a little while, as he's fucking me, I can close my eyes and be with Kenny again."

Her whispers turned to sobs as a year of misery, depression, and guilt broke free of the box in her head and overwhelmed her.

Camille pressed her closer, tried to calm her with soft words and caresses, but the anguish ran too deep.

Even a bit of composure was a long time coming, but when it did, Paula gently disengaged. Camille dragged the chair around the desk so they could sit knee-to-knee, as they did countless times while sharing whispered secrets about boys and men, school and work, love and life.

When she was sure Paula was again calm, she took her hands and said, "I am so angry with you I could spit! You carried all that around for a year all by yourself? What did you think I would do, disown you? Dissolve the business? What?"

"Hate me. You liked him. Everyone liked him. And I took him away from everyone. Permanently. How can you even look at me and not hate me now that you know?"

Camille shook her head. "I could no more hate you than I could hate myself. Now I want you to listen to me as I listened to you. Okay?"

"Okay."

"You. Did. Not. Kill. Kenny. Period. You surely have guilted yourself into believing it but it is simply not true. The sex may have pushed him over the edge at that particular moment, or it could have been the shower he took the next morning. Or it could have happened when he was driving to work and other people could have been killed, too. Did you hear *anything* the doctor told us after the autopsy?"

Paula shrugged.

"I should have realized and gone over it all with you again after the funeral. The aneurysm was so big, the wall so thin, that a sneeze could have caused it to burst. Those were the doctor's exact words."

"But if I hadn't been so weak and demanding and pushed him it might not have. He might have had another day or week or month. He might be still be alive today."

"So you're telling me you would have gone without sex all this time? That he'd never sneeze or blow his nose too hard or get angry? God, Paula, he died making love to you. Guys joke about wanting to go like that."

"But…"

"But nothing. You have to forgive yourself, not for killing him, but for letting him down. Do you think he would want you out getting drunk all the time, fucking strangers who picked you up in a bar? No effing way. If he could come back for five minutes he'd tell you to stop this shit and go find yourself a man as good as he was, someone gentle and kind who'll treat you the way you deserve, someone you can love the way you loved him. He'd want you to be happy, not miserable."

They talked for another hour and though Camille tried logic and reason and every sales technique she knew, when they finally parted, she knew Paula still blamed herself. Blame had become her life. And she didn't know what else she could do except stick by her and love her and help her whenever she could. Her demons had taken root and she would have to find a way to kill them before they killed her.

Paula unlocked the front door to the townhouse and wrinkled her nose at the stale odor. "When was the last time anyone showed this place?" she muttered, making a mental note to arrange for all vacant properties to be aired out at least once a week. A quick check of her watch assured her she had time, so she opened windows on the first floor then headed upstairs.

She was on her way back down when the doorbell rang.

"Mister Jeffries?"

"Yes, but please call me Dale."

"Dale, my name is Paula. Paula Romano. I believe you spoke with my partner yesterday?"

My god, he's gorgeous.

"I did, yes."

"Camille asked me to apologize. She's stuck at a closing that should have been completed over two hours ago. But I'm familiar with the condo, so why don't we have a look around."

And end up in the bedroom. Damn you wear that suit well.

When they reached the kitchen, she paged through the folder for the personal info page. "Oh. I should have asked. Will Mrs. Jeffries be joining us or are you screening alone?"

His crooked grin and warm chuckle sent a tingle

through her. "I'm afraid there is no Mrs. Jeffries. Just me."

"I'm sorry. This indicated you were married." She quickly fixed the form and made another mental note to talk to Camille about being careful which boxes she checked. "The room off the kitchen could be used as a dining room, a library, a media room, or an office. And there's a half bath off the hall."

As they toured the condo, Paula found herself thinking unprofessional thoughts about her client's perfectly-groomed brown hair, the hazel eyes that sparkled when he smiled, the firm backside he displayed when he bent over to pick up his dropped pen, and the graceful way he moved that told her he was in command of every finely tuned muscle in his body.

"May I be honest with you, Paula?" he asked as they stood in the master bedroom.

"Of course."

"This place is, what…twelve-hundred square feet?"

She consulted the listing sheet. "Wow. Pretty good. Twelve-sixty."

"I'm looking for something larger. Do you have any other listings you could show me?"

"Yes, but a thousand to thirteen hundred is what you'll find in this price range unless you want to look at least forty to fifty miles outside the city."

"And if we looked one hundred thousand dollars higher?"

"Sixteen to eighteen hundred feet."

"So another one-fifty would get us over two thousand square feet?"

She nodded. "But in that price range, you could look at houses in one of the surrounding towns. You'd get much more for your money and only be ten to fifteen minutes away from downtown."

"But there would be a yard and building to maintain."

"True, but the condo fee in town is likely to run seven to nine hundred dollars a month for what you want. That's eight to ten thousand dollars a year that could pay for a lawn and garden service and whatever tradesmen you might need, with money left over."

It was clear he never thought about a house, but was now running it all through his head. "And a yard would allow for a deck with a hot tub, a patio. You could show me some of these homes?"

"I can show you anything that's listed with the Multiple Listing Service, which is everything not being sold by owner. When would you like to see some?"

"I have all afternoon free. Perhaps you can show me some samples and then we can narrow it down from there for this weekend?"

You have no idea what I'd like to show you.

"I'll be happy to."

"You really talked him into a house?" Camille asked. She and Paula were relaxing in her office after hours.

"It looks that way. He followed me back here and I pulled up some properties to give him an idea about sizes and layouts and locations and by six he was convinced. He wants space, around twenty-five hundred feet, attached two or three car garage, some distance between him and his neighbors, and not brand new. He wants a home that feels lived in, the longer the better, and doesn't mind updating if it needs it."

"Geez, are you thinking what I'm thinking?"

"I'm thinking the Granderson place in Mayfield."

"Exactly!"

"But what to show him first? He'll need to see at least half a dozen places before that to be able to see the value in it."

They discussed strategy, searching MLS and

carefully crafting the showing tour to educate and, hopefully, close him on the Mayfield property. As they worked and talked and joked and laughed, Camille watched the time pass, growing happier with each passing hour, for they were hours that kept Paula out of the Klondike, away from booze, and out of a Bluelight Motel bed with some loser.

~ ~ ~

A few minutes after four o'clock Saturday afternoon, Paula turned her car into the long driveway of 147 Birchcrest Drive, the home of Quenton and Maria Granderson.

Dale let out a low whistle when he saw how far back from the street the rambling Victorian was set. "Is there no back yard at all?"

"If you don't mind, I'd rather you see for yourself. We can start with a walk around the outside."

An hour and twenty minutes later, having circled the house while exploring but a fraction of the four-acre lot, then touring the nine rooms, finished attic, and spacious basement, they stood at the bottom of the granite steps that led to the wrap-around front porch.

"Are you telling me I can buy this place for just a hundred and seventy-five thousand more than that townhouse you showed me the other day? What's the catch? Is it haunted? Is there a toxic waste dump under it?"

Paula's laugh filled the air. "The catches, plural, are that the lot has a deed restriction. It can never be subdivided."

"Lord, why would anyone want to? It's magnificent."

"I know. But you may not have noticed the other homes in this area have quarter- or half-acre lots. And you can buy one of those, in move-in condition, for a little less than the cost of that townhouse. This is the most expensive house in the area. Justifiably so, I think, but still, it needs fifty to a hundred thousand dollars in updates. When you're done, you'll have invested much more than the neighborhood, in general, warrants."

He looked startled. "That kind of honesty is not exactly the best sales technique."

"Dale, this place needs a special buyer. One who can appreciate its charm, its quirks, and its warts. Without the deed restriction, a developer would have snapped this up long ago, torn down the house, put in a road and built a dozen or more new homes."

"That would have been a shame."

"Hearing you say that makes me think you might be the special buyer the house has been waiting for."

"Is there any flexibility on the price."

"There's only one way to find out for sure."

I can't believe he's going to live in that huge house all by himself. And he wants to pay cash. Who does that these days? Maybe he's a drug dealer.

She signaled Frank, the bartender, for another double-vodka rocks.

Maybe he sold some Internet company for a zillion bucks. Who cares, I guess. As long as he shows up at the closing with certified checks.

"How are things tonight, Paula?" Frank asked as he swapped her empty glass for a new one and nearly filled it with Grey Goose instead of her usual Smirnoff. "You celebrating?"

"Sold a big one, Frank."

"That's great. Congrats."

She caught the tiny shake of his head as he walked away. He couldn't understand why an attractive, successful woman would come in so often, drink far too much, and leave with whatever guy happened to want to buy her a drink that night. But it was not his place to question what she did. He had his own problems. It was her business how she handled hers.

Her glass was only a quarter empty when three guys pushed through the front door talking and laughing as they settled at a table. She looked them over without staring, thinking any one of them would do, might even do her good enough to get her off.

As she sipped her drink, she noticed one kept glancing her way. And when hers was close to empty, he went up to the bar for more drinks and talked with Frank for a couple of minutes before resuming his seat. A minute later, Frank delivered another drink to her.

"From the guy in the blue shirt over there."

She threw back the rest of what was in her glass, then picked up the new one and looked his way as she held it up and took a sip. Then she smiled at him and watched as he told his friends, who did not appear to like the idea, that he was coming to join her.

He was tall and had friendly eyes under his short, dark hair. And a really great smile.

"Hi, I'm Eddie."

"Paula."

"Hi, Paula. May I join you?"

She shrugged and motioned to the next stool.

An hour and two more double-vodka-rocks later, Eddie put his arm around her waist as he guided her to her car. They leaned against it, making out for a few minutes until Paula felt the tingle.

"Let's go somewhere."

"Maybe I better drive," he said, taking the keys.

Once he settled her in the passenger seat and himself behind the wheel she said, "The Bluelight's a little way up the road."

He leaned over and kissed her again and the tingle

grew stronger.

"I don't want to go to a motel. I hate motels. I don't want a quickie. You are much too beautiful for that. I want to make it last for hours. I want drive to you wild. That takes time. My place is forty-five minutes away. Do you live closer?"

Paula never before brought any of the guys back to her house, but 'hours' and 'wild' kept echoing in her head and the tingle became demanding.

Once her front door closed behind them, he took her in his arms and kissed her. One hand caressed the back of her neck while the other pressed her close, close enough to feel his hardness pressing into her thigh. On unsteady legs, she led him to the bedroom, shedding her shoes along the way.

"God, you're so beautiful, so hot," he said again and again his words thrilled her. "I'm gonna make you feel so good. Will you strip for me?"

He sat on the edge of the unmade bed and watched as she shed her clothes, piece by piece, until only her panties remained. The way the room was moving, she wasn't sure how she managed to remain standing, but she took the three steps necessary to reach him. "You take these off," she said, "slow. I like it slow."

Eddie obliged her, hooking his fingers in the waist band and inching the black silk ever-so-slowly over her hips and down her thighs until he let go and they dropped to the floor.

His eyes met hers and again he told her how amazing she looked.

"Now you."

He helped her into the bed before walking around to the other side. He kicked off his shoes, shed his shirt, and let his trousers crumple to the floor.

When he moved to get into the bed, she slurred,

"Hey, you're not naked yet."

"I'm just going to keep some clothes on for a little while."

"What do you mean you're keeping your clothes on? How we gonna fuck if you're not naked?"

"I'm keeping them on for the moment. If we both get in bed naked, you won't be able to stop yourself from doing something, touching something that will get me going and then it will just turn into sex instead of something transcendent. You've trusted me enough to take your clothes off, trust me enough to let me leave mine on for awhile."

The alcohol fog made it difficult to figure out exactly what he meant, but she knew she wanted to be with him and nodded.

"Good. This is a very special technique that was taught to me almost a year ago."

He slid under the covers and stretched out on his side, facing her, and pulled her into a close embrace.

"Empty your mind. Just feel the closeness of our bodies. Feel the warmth. Don't think about it, just feel it. Relax your body and your mind and if you start to feel something odd or strange, that will be our auras, our souls touching, connecting."

He began lightly stroking her, whispering so softly, the words barely registered. After awhile, the stroking stopped. A bit later, the words faded to silence. And some time later he could tell from her breathing it was time.

~ ~ ~

Paula awoke at the urging of her screaming bladder. Her head throbbed -- no surprise there -- but she felt oddly refreshed, not at all like she usually felt when she awoke at the Bluelight. Despite her bladder's insistence, she took a full minute to open her eyes a hair-width at a time, having too often in the past snapped them open only to have the daylight add another layer of pain. When they opened enough to see, she realized where she was. Her arm reached out, but the bed was empty, another non-surprise.

With a sigh, she threw back the covers and walked naked into her bathroom.

What the hell happened last night?

She was worried because she couldn't remember anything after he climbed into bed with her and held her.

What did he do to me? Drug me or something?

Her fingers reached down to explore, front and back, but nothing hurt, nothing felt different. She stood and looked in the mirror but to her surprise she saw only herself, not the drunken tramp who usually appeared the morning after. And she felt good, despite the hangover. And even that wasn't as bad as usual.

"What the hell did you do to me last night?" Her reflection just shook its head and shrugged.

Two aspirin and two glasses of water were followed by a warm shower. When she emerged from the bathroom toweling her hair, she glanced at the bedside clock and did a double-take. It was after noon.

Ohmygod, how can it be so late? Could I have slept ten freaking hours or more?

She dashed through the living room into the foyer, found her bag on the small table where she'd dropped it last night, and dug out her phone.

"It's about time," Camille said, not bothering with a hello. "Your twelve o'clock arrived early. Where are you?"

"Cam, I'm sorry. I way overslept. Is there any chance you can cover for me. Tell them I'm having car trouble. Their file is on my desk. The showings are all set. I'll explain later. I want to explain later."

When she closed her phone and dragged her bag off

the table, a paper fell to the floor. It was folded and had her name on it but the tile was too cold to stand around on naked, so she carried it back to the bedroom and sat on the side of the bed before unfolding it.

Paula,

I know what we shared together last night was probably unlike anything that ever happened to you with someone you just met, but I hope you enjoyed the experience as much as I did. I had a good time with you at the bar and when we got back to your place, well, mere words cannot do it justice as I'm sure you know.

I wish I could see you again tomorrow (or today, I guess) but I'm leaving today and am not sure when I'll return. But I'll try to remember to send you a postcard.

Thank you again. I hope to see you soon, but whether we get together again or not, I will never forget our night together.

Eddie

Camille handed back the note and said, "Well it certainly sounds like you two did *something*."

"I know. But what? He didn't come inside me. I checked."

"So he used a condom."

"If he did, he took it with him, wrapper and all, because I checked the trash in the bedrooms, the bathrooms, and the kitchen and it wasn't there."

"Maybe he did slip you a roofie."

"No. I felt too damn good this morning. And he was never alone with my drinks. The one time I went to pee I took it with me."

Camille wrinkled her nose at the thought but said nothing.

"Then all I can think of is that the sex was so damn good it short-circuited your brain or something. Or maybe the alcohol did."

"But I can remember everything, even him holding me and whispering and touching me. As drunk as I was, when he said the thing about our auras and souls I remember thinking he might be a little nuts but I swear, Cam, I remember feeling something, like something peaceful going though me. And that's it. A total blank after that until I woke up."

"I don't know what to say. But I do know I'd be waiting pretty damn impatiently for him to get back from wherever he went so we could have a repeat engagement, but without the booze."

~ ~ ~

The following two weeks were exceptional for three reasons. First, Dale Jeffries arranged for all the usual inspections to be conducted in one day, Tuesday, and three days later, he, the Grandersons, their respective attorneys, and Paula sat in a room as monies were paid and the title transferred. Neither Paula nor Camille had ever heard of a sale taking less than a week from first showing to closing, but they learned that if enough money changed hands, almost anything could be accomplished.

The second thing was the partnership securing nine accepted offers on in-house listings, four by Paula and five by Camille, cutting their listing inventory in half.

And third, for the longest stretch since Kenny died, Paula did not once see the inside of the Klondike. Part of the reason was how busy she was with all the various deals. The other part was the Eddie Enigma, as she and Camille began to call it.

Discovering what happened during her blackout period became an obsession of sorts. At first, she tried drink. She settled onto the sofa with a bucket of ice, a bottle of Grey Goose, and a glass and drank until the room started to spin. She had hoped the booze would unblock her brain. It didn't.

Next, she tried meditation, both tipsy and sober. Then one double shot nursed for hours. She tried reading, cleaning, music, and relaxation with a white-noise generator, but nothing worked. She ran out of ideas by the second Saturday after Eddie and spent the evening half-watching *P.S. I Love You* and *Groundhog Day* and half thinking about him, how they talked and laughed in the bar, how aroused she was on the drive to her house, and how gently he held her before whatever happened happened.

It wasn't until the following Tuesday she realized she only thought about Kenny a few times since the night with Eddie. She searched inside herself and found the guilt still there but not the need to forget and remember. The next afternoon, Dale Jeffries called to ask her to dinner on Friday to thank her for helping him find his new home. His words were strictly business, but his tone hinted at something more.

~ ~ ~

"This is a bad idea. I'm not ready to date."

"It's not a date," Camille said, "It's a thank-you meal. He's happy he's going to be living in a beautiful, grand old home surrounded by gorgeous, private grounds instead of some sterile, partitioned box in the city and he wants to show his gratitude to the person who made it happen. If you were a guy, would you think it was date?"

"I guess you're right. It's just my insecurities getting the better of me. What would a guy like that want with some real estate broker anyway. With his looks and money, he probably has a little black book full of women. You're right. It was just my imagination."

"Any breakthroughs with the Eddie Enigma?"

Paula shook her head. "I keep thinking about him but I'm resigned to waiting until he comes back."

She saw the look in Camille's eyes and knew what put it there. "My feelings about what I did to Kenny haven't changed, Cam, but I haven't felt the urge to visit the Klondike. Whatever happened with Eddie that night must have been so amazing, some part of my brain decided no bar pickup is likely to ever match it."

Her faced clouded. "I hope this Eddie thing hasn't ruined sex for me. I mean, what if it really did tweak something in my head and I'll never enjoy regular sex again?"

Camille spent a few seconds in silent debate, deciding how to ask the question. "*Have* you been enjoying sex?"

She watched Paula blush, which was the last reaction she had expected.

"You know I haven't. Not since Kenny."

"I can't believe you just admitted that. Now *I'm* starting to wonder what the hell Eddie *did* do to you."

"Whatever it was, it's all I can think about. Well, not all, but you know what I mean."

Camille nodded. "And you really haven't been to…"

"Not since that night."

"That's incredible! God, Paula, I'm so happy to hear that."

"Look, don't get all worried about never enjoying sex again. I'm sure that under the right circumstances, it will be as wonderful as it always was. And hey, who knows, maybe if things go well at dinner tonight, you'll get the chance to find out."

"You're joking, right?"

Dale did a fine impersonation of someone hurt at not being believed. "Would you have believed me if I told you when I signed the offer that we'd close the deal in a week? Oh, wait. I did tell you and if memory serves, you asked the same question." His grin displayed toothpaste-commercial white teeth to accompany his laughing eyes.

Paula felt a familiar flutter, one that tickled her chest each time he grinned like that, a flutter she hadn't felt for a very long time. "You actually hired a designer who redecorated that huge house, complete with furnishings, in just two weeks? And updated the bathrooms? And the kitchen?"

"And the wiring and plumbing. But if I'm to be completely accurate, she also acted as a general contractor and had a team of four, plus herself, and of course, the tradesmen, working on it nearly round-the-clock."

"Well, there you go. That makes all the difference. That's only about two rooms each."

Their laughs connected midway across the candlelit table.

When he asked her to dinner, she had no idea he would be taking her to *Cena Bella*. When he told her their destination in the car, she said a silent thank you the guardian angel who caused her to choose the dress and heels over the pantsuit and flats.

The restaurant, the staff, and especially the food were even better than she expected. It was the place she and Kenny always talked about, dreamed of eating at, but never seemed to be able to save enough to actually afford. Now, here she was, sitting a mere thirty-six inches away from a man who would probably hand over his credit card without bothering to look at the check with those dreamy, hypnotic eyes that never seemed to wander away from her.

"I suppose you're right. One room per week per person is not as amazing as I thought. But they did do a great job. Would you like a tour of the house after dinner?"

Her heart skipped a beat as excitement and dread

fought for command of her emotions.

Is this an invitation to a house tour, or something more? Only one way to find out. Steady now.

"I would, thank you. I've been curious what you've done with it."

Half an hour later, after sharing an aptly named a Chocolate Raspberry Explosion — a chocolate chunk fudge brownie dipped in white chocolate, then dipped in dark chocolate, sandwiched between layers of double-chocolate cake, and topped with a rich, intense raspberry sauce — they were headed out of the city. Soft jazz filled the car. They had talked almost non-stop from the time he picked her up, sharing bits and pieces of themselves. Now they shared silence, to see how that fit.

She glanced over, admiring his profile, wondering what would happen once they were alone in his house. Part of her wanted him to want her tonight, wanted to be with him, but not just for sex. She wanted to make love, even if it was just for one night. She could sense he would be strong and gentle, would care about her needs and not rush to satisfy himself like the men she gave herself to for so long. But another part was scared, frightened of what might happen inside her head.

When the car pulled into the driveway, a series of low lanterns turned on to illuminate the driveway as floodlights chased the dark from the parking area, garage, and around the house.

"The outside lighting looks very nice."

"Thank you. I wanted the lights around the house, but the driveway lights were the designer's idea."

The sounds of the night tickled her ears as they walked from the driveway to the front door. The few times she showed the property were all during the day when the distant sound of children playing, dogs barking, and vehicles passing made up the bulk of the background noise. When they reached the bottom of the steps, she touched his arm, stopped, and closed her eyes to enjoy the symphony of amorous insects mixed with the scurrying of small critters.

After a minute, she released a short sigh and said, "When I was a child, we lived in the country. My mom told me the night sounds were nature playing music to help us relax and sleep. We moved to the city when I was eleven after my dad lost his job and it took me months to get used to falling asleep to the city noises."

Dale gave a small grunt. "I've been here half-a-dozen times at night these past two weeks and I never stopped to listen. It is soothing in a way. I guess I'll find out just how soothing later on. Tonight will be my first night sleeping here. Thankfully, it will be in my own bed, so I won't have to get used to that, too." He chuckled as they crossed the porch to the door. "The decorator wanted to get me a new bedroom set, one in keeping with the period of the house, but I was determined *that* room of furniture would not change.

"I told the decorator I wanted the house to look as it might have when it was built, with the exception of the kitchen and the bathrooms, though you'll see she managed to bring them up-to-date while retaining a period look. She even managed to pull it off in my bedroom."

Paula was both amazed and charmed by the transformation that took place in a mere two weeks. When she stepped into the wide foyer, she felt as if she stepped onto an early-1900s-era movie set. The feeling stayed with her through the living room, parlor, and dining room. It was not until they passed into the kitchen that she returned to the twenty-first century. But then he led her up the gleaming, curved, walnut staircase and she was back in the past. Each bedroom was decorated to highlight its particular charms. Even the master, with Dale's solid cherry contemporary set, managed a vintage feel.

As they descended the stairs, he asked, "Would you like a glass of wine or something else? I've been looking forward to my first fire in the parlor fireplace and would very much like to share it with you, if you don't need to hurry home."

He wants me to stay. He wants me. But he gives me an obvious out if I want it. Quite the gentleman. But do I want this? Can I do it without...stop!.

"I think a fire and a glass of wine would be lovely."

"Great. Let me get it started, then I'll have to run downstairs. I haven't brought anything up from the cellar yet."

When he was satisfied the kindling was burning well, he opened the doors of a tall, antique cabinet and turned on a stereo. Then he excused himself. Paula walked around, examining artwork and decorations, imagining what it would be like to live in this beautiful home that made her condo look like a middle-class holding pen.

"Here we go," she heard from behind her.

She turned to find him holding a glass in each hand, wearing that grin that kept melting her inside. He motioned for her to join him on the leather sofa that faced the fireplace.

"For weeks, I've been imagining myself sitting here tonight with a glass of wine and a good book. I never dreamed the book would be replaced by a lovely woman. By the way, have I mentioned how amazing you look in that dress?"

"Not more than two or three times." Her pleasure at the repetition was clear, as was the need to sit before her rapidly weakening knees gave out.

He pursed his lips and shook his head in mock dismay. "My memory seems to be failing me in the presence of such beauty and charm."

She gave a little cough. "If you keep this up you're going to need a trowel."

His laugh filled the room and sent her flutters into overdrive. "Sorry. I *was* laying it on a bit thick. But I meant every word of it. Tell me, now that the deal has closed, am I still considered a client?"

"A former client."

"Good. So you can tell me all the little secrets real estate brokers never share outside the profession."

"But if I did that, wouldn't I be sharing secrets outside the profession?"

This time, they both laughed as they settled on the sofa and let the flames hypnotize them for a few minutes until Paula broke the spell.

"I had a very nice time tonight, Dale. Thank you for the wonderful meal."

"You're welcome. But I should be thanking you for agreeing to be seen with me. I don't often get to spend an evening with a woman of your caliber."

"Oh, go on. A man in your position must have his choice of women of all shapes, sizes, and ages."

"It's true. I do. But invariably their interest is in what I can do for them or what they can get from me. With us, it was just business." He noticed a flush spreading across her face and tilted his head. "Wasn't it just business?"

Oh god, why did he have to ask me that?

"As far as you know it was, indeed, all business."

He grinned and stared and she knew she'd admit the truth in the end so she might as well get it over with.

"The first time I met you, as we were touring that condo, I might have had some un-businesslike thoughts about you."

"Ah ha! Care to share some details?"

"No."

"Fair enough." He glanced at the fireplace. "Excuse

me for a minute."

He grabbed a poker and moved the wood around a bit. When he returned, he stood in front of her and asked, "Would you like to dance?"

His right hand enfolded hers while his left landed at her waist. Over the next few minutes, the six inches of space that separated them at the start slowly shrank to zero. Her head rested on his shoulder as her breasts pressed softly against his chest. His scent made her light-headed and she felt as if she was floating across the floor in his arms. He was so strong, so warm, and it had been so very long since a man held her like this.

She turned her head up with a smile and he brushed his lips across hers. It was enough to send a shock to her center and she pressed closer as their lips met again. The heat of his kiss, his tongue, and his body made her swoon and he scooped her into his arms and carried her to the sofa. An image of Kenny carrying her to bed flashed behind her eyes. She squeezed them shut and drove it from her mind. Then she silently begged.

Please. I just want one night. Please let me have one night.

He sat and cradled her as their tongues resumed their explorations. One arm continued to hold her while the hand on the other caressed her cheek and stroked her hair. His lips moved to her neck, searching for the spot they seemed to know would be there. And when they found it, a long, low moan let them know. His fingernails trailed down her cheek and her neck to her chest and brushed along the curve of her breast raking the nipple through the thin fabrics of her dress and bra. Again she moaned. Her hand mimicked his but didn't stop at his chest. It moved lower and lower until it found his rigid manhood. Her fingernails scratched across his trousers eliciting a sigh of sublime pleasure.

His hand moved lower, across her stomach when suddenly the specter returned. She stiffened and whispered, "No, no! Not now, please!" Her head shook, desperately trying to drive away the images of Kenny, but to no avail. "You ruined it. You ruined it!" she cried as tears began to fall.

"Paula, what's wrong? Did I hurt you?"

She slid off him and curled herself at the other end of the sofa. "I'm sorry, Dale. I'm so sorry. I…" Frustration threatened to overwhelm her but she fought it back, determined not to make any more of a scene. "I'm sorry. You didn't do anything. You were wonderful. You are wonderful. I…"

What can I tell him?

"My husband died almost a year ago. We were…together when it happened. I loved him so much it almost killed me. I…I thought I was ready to be with someone again after all this time, but the ghosts are still haunting me. I wanted to be with you tonight, I wanted it so much, but I can't. I just can't."

Tears began to flow again. Dale slid across the sofa, opened his arms and said, "It's okay, Paula. Come. Cry. Let it out."

She smiled through her sobs, moved into his embrace, and buried her head against his chest as her tears slowly drained her anger and humiliation.

~ ~ ~

When he dropped her off that night, Dale told her he would call. She hoped, but didn't really expect him to, and twenty-one days of silence fulfilled her expectation.

"I can't really blame him, Cam. No guy like him is going to waste time on damaged goods."

"God, I wish you'd stop saying that. You are not damaged. You're hurt. There's a big difference. And you're getting better. It's been over a month since you had a drink if you don't count the glass-and-a-half of wine you had that night with him. You were hurting for almost a year. You can't expect it all to vanish in a few weeks."

"I know, Cam. It will take time. I just don't know how I'll know when the time is up. I was so embarrassed, so humiliated that night. I don't think I could stand going through that again. So I'm not going to try. I have work and you and that's enough for the next year or two or three. I'm swearing off men. Kenny included. No more sitting around pining for a dead man no matter how much I loved him. See. I said loved. Past tense."

"Oh stop. You're always going to love him, even when you're married again with ten kids. He'll always have a place in your heart, sweetie, but after enough time has passed, he won't consume you as he's been doing. You'll know when that time comes. And that's when you'll start living a full life again."

~ ~ ~

Paula tossed her bag on the sofa and stretched. It had been a long, but fruitful Saturday. The two condos she sold would pay for the two-week Bahamas cruise she and Camille were planning when Christmas rolled around in a few months. The second sale was the unit she showed to Dale Jeffries so long ago.

Though he never did call, she thought of him now and then, sometimes with regret, sometimes with pride at how far she felt she had come emotionally since that wonderful, then awful night.

The first thing she did when she reached the kitchen was grab a marker and put a thick X through today's date. "Has it really been four months?" she asked the calendar. "I guess so."

As she popped the mac and cheese frozen dinner in the microwave, she wondered how Dale was doing in his new home and if he ever finished that huge attic into the billiard room he wanted. Then she wondered what kind of woman he might be with, but after a minute's speculation, shrugged and said, "Who cares."

While the oven did its thing, she poured a glass of vanilla soy milk, set the table with a fork and napkin, and leaned against the counter to watch the numbers count down to zero.

The loud, piercing beeps sounded different, odd, as if they were trying to be a bell tone. A pot holder helped her slide the plastic tray onto her dish and as she placed it on the table, the door bell rang.

Oh! that's what it was.

She glanced at the clock.

Who's showing up unannounced after eight-thirty?

When she reached the front door, she looked through the peep hole and rocked back in surprise.

Him? Really? After all this time?

She pulled open the door.

"Hello, Eddie."

"Hello, Paula. I'm sorry I never sent you that post card."

She laughed. "I forgot all about that. Would you like to come in? I have a few questions I'd like to ask you."

"I was hoping you'd ask."

She led him into the kitchen. "I was just about to eat my gourmet mac and cheese. Care to share?"

"Actually, I love mac and cheese. But I don't want to take your dinner."

"That's okay. I usually only eat half of it, so I can keep this girlish figure."

"In that case, yes please."

"Something to drink?"

"Water's good."

She set a place for him, scooped half the mac and cheese into his dish, then grabbed a bottle of water from the fridge and poured it into his glass.

They watched each other take a few bites, washing each down with a sip from their glasses. Finally, Eddie said, "You really do look wonderful. I'm happy to see you're not drinking anymore, at least not like you used to."

"And what makes you think that?"

It wasn't quite a smile and wasn't quite a grin, but the look on his face made her feel happy.

"Do you remember how you looked the night I met you?"

She shrugged and shook her head.

"Well, I do. You looked like a woman who'd seen the empty bottom of far too many shot glasses. There's no way you could still be drinking and look as great as you do now."

Paula felt herself blushing.

"And with that color in your cheeks, you look even more beautiful. But you said you had questions"

"Yes, I do. What the effing hell did you do to me that night we spent together?"

"We slept together."

"I know that. But I can't remember a damn thing after you were holding me. Nothing, until I woke up the next morning."

"How did you feel when you woke up?"

She started, her face filled with curiosity. "Why do I get the feeling you already know the answer?"

It was his turn to shrug.

"I was hung over a little. But even so, I felt wonderful. Refreshed. And I slept for over ten hours straight. That just doesn't happen. So I repeat the question, what did you do to me? Did you slip me some kind of drug? Did we f…did we have sex?"

"I promise I'll tell you, but first, I need to tell you a

story. But before the story, would you mind if I act like a guy for a minute?"

"Uhhh...okay."

Eddie grinned, picked up his plate, and shoved the rest of the mac and cheese into his mouth.

Paula laughed as he chewed and swallowed. "That *is* gross, but *very* guy-like."

After he washed the last of it down, he began.

"When I left here last time, I packed and took off on a road trip around the country, visiting and staying with, or near, family and friends. I needed to make amends for the way I treated them all after I killed my wife."

Paula jumped in her seat, shock and fear registering on her face and in her eyes.

He noticed and said, "I'm sorry. That was a little too dramatic. I didn't actually kill her, but I believed I was responsible for her death.

"Jen and I were party people. We enjoyed having fun and booze was always part of the fun. Normally, one or the other of us would take it easy, be the designated driver if you will. But the night she died, we were at a party less than a mile from our place. It was her turn to let go but after a few drinks she began telling me I should have more, too. That it was such a short drive home on a back road that gets almost no traffic and we could just go slow. So I did and we had a great time with all our friends.

"On the ride home, I was going slow, maybe twenty-five or thirty miles an hour. I knew the road like I knew my own face and was ready when we came to the sharp left. I took my foot off the gas and went to brake but my foot glanced off the edge of the brake pedal and jammed down on the gas. We shot forward, through the guardrail, and down into a shallow ravine."

He shuddered before taking a deep breath. "When we crashed into the tree that stopped us, the windshield was shattered and Jen was impaled by a broken tree branch that had poked right through the airbag into her chest. She cried for me to help her but I was dazed from hitting my head on the side window several times. Even if I'd been sober, there was nothing I could have done. The branch clipped her heart and as I sat trapped by my seat belt and branches, I watched her die. I couldn't even free my hand enough to touch her, or comfort her as her life bled away.

"I remember screaming when her head finally slumped forward and I must have passed out because the next thing I remember is daylight and someone yelling. It was mid-morning and the alcohol was no longer dulling my senses. My whole body throbbed with pain and then I remembered and looked over and screamed again."

He paused for a long drink of water.

"I never admitted I was drinking. I didn't need the state to punish me. I spent the next year and a half punishing myself. I lost my job and my friends, cut off contact with my family, and started relationships with vodka, scotch, and other assorted distilled spirits. It was the only way I could forget what I'd done. It was my responsibility to protect her that night and I failed. I willingly put both of us at risk and she died crying for me to help her. Booze was the only thing that made me forget.

"That's what you were doing in the Klondike that night and all the nights before that, right? Trying to forget?"

She wanted to say something, anything, but all she could do was nod.

"And the sex, that was so you could be with Kenny again in your head."

This time, the words came. "How do you know that? And about Kenny?"

"I know about the drinking and sex because that's

what I was doing. As for Kenny, remember the last time we met? Shortly before I came over to you? I was at the bar getting more drinks for my friends and was talking to the bartender. I was asking about you. I was asking because...do you remember the first time you went to the Klondike?"

"Not really."

"Do you remember the guy you came on to, who took you to the Bluelight. Room 27."

Her eyes widened with understanding. "That was you?"

"I'm ashamed to admit it was. While we were, uhh, together, you said, 'Faster, Kenny, faster' and a couple of similar things. So when I saw you sitting in that same seat, what, nine or ten months later, I asked the bartender about you and who Kenny was."

"But why? And we're back to my original question again. What did you do to me?"

"I'll get to that soon. But back to that first night we were together. As drunk as I was, and as poorly as I'm sure I performed, I never forgot you."

He laughed. "Yeah, I don't blame you for looking like that. I wouldn't believe a line like that either. But it's true. You see, that night, I was, in a sense, your first, but you were my last."

"I was your last? You mean you haven't had sex with anyone since that night?"

"That's it."

"Did you find God or something?"

"No. I found myself."

He laughed again at her reaction. "Every answer leads to another question, doesn't it?"

"It seems that way. Are you going to tell me how you found yourself?"

"The same way you're in the process of finding

yourself, I think. A few nights after our first encounter, I was in a hotel bar and hit on this woman, a girl, really, who couldn't have been more than twenty-one or twenty-two. She said her name was Darla. It must have been clear to her how much I'd already had to drink but she led me to a table and started talking with me. I honestly don't remember what we talked about, but she must have learned enough to figure out why I was really there.

"She invited me up to her room, undressed me and got me into bed, then stripped to her underwear and climbed in beside me. I made the same protest you did and received the same answer you did. Then she put her arms around me and did for me what I did for you.

"I thought it was dumb at first, but then I started to feel something passing from her to me, a warmth…something, and I began to feel a sense of peace for the first time since the accident. So I went with it. And the next thing I remember is waking up around noon the next day feeling great. It was like a switch had been thrown in my brain. She was gone, of course, but had folded my clothes and left a note on top. I tried to find out who she was, but the desk wouldn't give me any info at all and I decided it wasn't important, that I'd think of her as an angel of some kind sent to rescue me.

"I forgave myself as I knew Jen would have wanted me to. I cleaned myself up and swore off booze until I got my life back on track again. It took me a while, but I did and all that time I kept thinking about you. How much fun you were just to talk to. But there was more. At least I thought so. Maybe it was just my besotted imagination, but I sensed something special about you.

"Anyway, the last time we met was my first time out with the guys since I changed. It was my challenge to myself to drink two beers and no more. I became concerned that my too-long spell of heavy drinking turned me into an alcoholic. I'd not had a drink since that night with the girl and I had to find out if I could control myself.

"I suggested we go to the Klondike because I was hoping to run into you. Well, hoping and fearing. If you were still getting drunk and picking up guys I wasn't sure what I'd do. There was no way I wanted to get drawn back into that life. But then, there you were, and you didn't seem to recognize me. So I decided to try to help you the way Darla helped me.

"Honestly, I was afraid it wouldn't work. I didn't remember exactly what she said, just that the words were soft and pleasant and calming. And when *she* did it, it was a selfless act. She didn't have an ulterior motive. I did. I really wanted to get to know you better, but not the drunk Paula, the real one."

"So here we are. That's my story and I'm sticking to it."

Shell-shocked was the best way to describe how Paula looked and felt at that moment. "But you still haven't told me what you did to me that night. Why I can't remember what we did."

"I know. Here's the thing. I can't really explain it. I can only do it."

"Yeah, but I don't have casual sex anymore.

"I know. It ended when you stopped drinking."

"How do you know that?"

"The same way I knew you stopped drinking. Look, granted you were drunk at the time, but you trusted me once before. And look at how that turned out. So I'm asking you to trust me one more time. Will you do that?"

Paula's head spun with hows and whys and what-ifs.

In a way, he did change my life. But I was drunk then. What's he going to do? How can I trust him? Can I really strip in front of him sober? Do I even want to? But that morning-after was so wonderful. Can he really make me feel that way again? But what if he hurts me? But he won't. He didn't before. And his eyes are so kind, his whole demeanor so peaceful. And he likes me. And I was ready to jump into bed with Dale that time. But I swore off men. Oh, god, what if I say yes and it happens again? But it didn't happen last time.

"You can really make me feel the way I did the last time we were together?"

"I'll do my best."

"Do I have to get drunk again?"

"God no! I told you. I want to get to know the real Paula." His hands splayed out before him. "This Paula."

She sat and stared at him for a minute, trying to take his measure. Then she gathered her fork, dish, and glass, and carried them to the sink. On the way, she saw him start to gather his and she waved him to remain seated, though she was happy to see his willingness to pitch in.

One point.

She returned for his stuff, scraped and emptied it all, and put everything in the dishwasher. Then she turned and smiled and crooked her finger, using it to call him to her.

His eyes were full of hope as he approached and stopped a hand's-length away from her.

"Kiss me," she said softly.

So he did. He leaned forward and it was soft, and warm, and full of promise. But most of all, she felt the flutter.

Two points.

"Come on," she said.

She took his hand and led him to her bedroom, motioning him to one side of the bed while she stationed herself on the other.

"Is there a particular order in which we have to get undressed?"

His soft chuckle warmed her. "I don't think it matters."

"Okay. Then you can get started."

He reached for the top button of his shirt as she turned and walked to her bureau. She opened the drawer as she looked over her shoulder and said, "I'm not getting naked."

He made a fist and banged his stomach with it as he said, "Oh, darn! I was so looking forward to that." Then he laughed and said, "I expected that would be the case."

Three points.

She returned to the bed with a long tee shirt. He was clad now only in his own tee and boxers. "Turn around, please," she said and he did.

She kicked off her shoes, pulled her shirt over her head, and began to unfasten her pants. That's when she noticed their reflections in the window. The darkness outside had transformed it into a mirror. She could see him clearly and he could see her if he had been looking, but he must have realized before she did and averted his eyes downward.

Ten points! Bingo!

At that moment, all her worries and fears about him vanished. She envied him his peace, his having moved past his pain and guilt and looked forward to the day when she would be in the same place. Maybe he *could* help.

She wiggled out of her pants, stripped off her knee-highs, unhooked her bra, and pulled the tee on. Her panties remained on. She was not sure if they would have sex tonight, but if they did, she still found it sexier for the guy to take them off.

"Okay, Eddie. What next?"

"The light?"

"Right!"

She padded over to flip the switch, then stood for a moment to let her eyes get used to the dark. When she could see well enough, she returned to the bed and slid in to find Eddie already under the covers on his side.

"Can I kiss you good night," she asked, "or would that spoil things."

"I'm not sure. Let's find out."

They both moved to the center of the bed until she was again in his arms, as she had been the last time. Their lips found each other for a short, sweet, lip cuddle. Then he began gently stroking her and whispering, but this time he stopped after a minute.

"I'm sorry. I forgot to tell you one very important thing."

"What's that?" she murmured.

He resumed his gentle stroking.

"Tomorrow morning, when you wake up, I'll still be here."

The Klutz

Sandi suspected what was coming when Maury called her into the office. It had not been a good day and she felt it was about to get worse.

She knocked and pushed the door open when she heard, "Come."

Maury was seated behind his desk. On the desk in front of him, in the middle of a green desk pad, sat a white envelope.

Yup. It is definitely about to get worse. Maybe a good offense?

"Maury, I'm really sorry about the dishes. I just got startled when Jake yelled when he burned himself and…"

Maury held up a hand. "Sandi, you're a real nice girl. You're bright and personable and you try real hard, but you're a klutz. Restaurant and klutz just don't mix. There are just too many things to break, too many ways to get hurt." He picked up the envelope. "I'm sorry, kid, but I have to let you go."

Everyone was kind about saying goodbye, but she could see the relief in their eyes. She began working there three days, a dozen or so dishes, a bunch of glasses, several meals, two pies, and a tray of just-fried eggplant ago, and it was clear the rest of the staff were happy not to have to wonder what klutz-caused disaster would happen next.

She walked the two blocks to the bus stop and settled onto the bench. This time of day, the bus ran once an hour so she had at least a thirty-minute wait.

Three days. Two and a half, really. That's a new record. I guess I should have realized food service wouldn't be a clumsy-proof career.

She pulled her Kindle from her bag and lost herself in the trials and tribulations of Agents Cherry Valentine and Dirk Woodsman as they struggled to stop the evil Doctor Magma without being distracted by their mutual, simmering passion. Just as they were about to fall into Magma's carefully-laid trap in Iceland, a car stopped and a voice called out, "Hey, gorgeous. Want a ride?"

She glanced up and said, "Thank you, but I don't accept rides from strange men in convertibles."

"Come on. I'm a nice guy. I'll buy you candy and ice cream."

"Oh! Well, why didn't you say so in the first place?"

She dropped the Kindle in her bag and hurried to the curb.

"Say, you could be a masher or something and I'm just a sweet, innocent girl. How do I know I'll be safe with you?"

"Because if anything happens to you, your insane brother will kick my ass from here to your house and back again. Then my wife will murder me in my sleep."

They both laughed as she slid into the front seat and leaned over to plant a peck on his cheek.

"Thanks for stopping, Barry. How's Angie?"

"Fine. Nothing ever changes when you're married. Say, what are you doing out here at this time of day?"

She turned a deep breath into a dramatic sigh. "I got fired. Again."

"Ouch. That's the second time this month, isn't it?"

She nodded. "And it's only the second week."

He pointed his car toward her house while she recounted her most recent employment failure.

"I don't know what to do, Barry. It's like my brain is disconnected from the rest of me. I'm never going to save enough money to go to dental hygienist school if I keep getting fired after a few days." She sighed and made a rude noise. "It would probably be a waste of money anyway. Even if I graduated, what dentist is going to hire a clumsy dope?"

"Sandi, you're not a dope. But you *are* the clumsiest human being I have ever known. I used to hear stories about you when you were in middle school. I used to think the kids were exaggerating or making up stuff to be funny. Then Trane and I got friendly when we both made the basketball team and I met you and I felt like looking up all those middle school kids and apologizing."

His quick glance caught the horror on her face. "Come on. You mean you didn't know kids were making fun of you back then? I can't believe Trane never said anything."

She shook her head. "I knew some kids made fun, but I didn't know the whole school knew."

"Seriously? I mean, did a day ever go by when you didn't drop or bump into or knock over or trip over something?"

A second glance confirmed it. "Look, Dee, you're twenty years old and you've been out of school for what, fourteen months and how many jobs have you lost? Ten, fifteen?"

"I stopped counting at twenty."

"Cripes! Don't you think it's time you did something about it? I don't know what, but there has to be some therapy, some program to help you."

~ ~ ~

Sandi looked up from her Kindle at the sound of the front door opening.

"Hey, brat. Knock anyone over today?"

She rolled her eyes and made an unladylike gesture.

Older brothers can be so *annoying.*

"What are you doing here this close to suppertime, as if I didn't know. Dad told Mom last week they should have named you Mooch instead of Trane."

They flung insults back and forth for a few minutes until both were laughing. Then he grabbed her arm and dragged her out of the chair to her feet for a hug.

"How are you really doing, brat? Mom told me you got fired again?"

A quick synopsis of her brief affair with food service left him shaking his head. "Barry didn't tell me he gave you a ride home yesterday."

"Why would he? Are you a girl or something? You have to know every detail of your best friend's life?"

"When it involves my little sister I do."

Further argument was forestalled by the ringing of the house phone. "Sandi," their mother called from the kitchen, "it's Angie for you."

She picked up the extension and said, "Hi. Why are you calling me on my parent's phone?"

"Because half the time you forget where your phone is, and half of the rest of the time it's either broken because you dropped it or dead because you forgot to charge it."

Sandi sighed. It was true. "So what's up?"

"Barry told me what happened yesterday. I'm sorry. But last night, we had dinner with Jess and Zack Timlin, some friends from college. While we were eating, Barry remembered to tell me he saw you and what happened, and we all sort of got to talking about you and your…ahh…difficulty. Well, Jess thinks she can help you fix the problem if you're willing to work at it."

"How? Is she a doctor or something?"

"No. Actually, she entertains at kids' parties. She didn't say how she could help, but she said she had a similar problem when she was young and she's pretty sure she can."

"I don't know, Ange. It sounds kind of odd to me."

"I know, but if she really can help…I mean, it wouldn't hurt to talk to her. She and Zack live in Centerville. How about I come with you on Saturday. She's really nice and I'll drive so you won't even have to take the bus.

"And hey, just imagine. If she *can* turn things around, you might even start driving!"

~ ~ ~

"We're almost there now, so will you please calm down," Angie said as she turned onto Washburn Ave. "Why are you so nervous?"

"I don't know," Sandi replied. "I just am." She paused for a long sigh. "I guess…I've been this way all my life. I hate it, but it's who I am, who I've always been. If so big a part of me changes, what if all the rest of me changes, too? I like the rest of me. I don't want it to change."

"Sandi, being clumsy is *not* who you are. It's a problem, like stuttering. You are who you are despite the problem and you'll remain who you are without it unless you *choose* to change. You're sweet and kind and funny, and it's not because you trip and drop stuff. It's because you have a wonderful heart and brain. Fixing how you move and whatever isn't going to change that. Now take a deep breath and relax, because we're here."

"I've been looking forward to meeting you," Jessica told Sandi after introductions were made. Then she turned to Angie and said, "Pamela Tiffin."

Sandi's look of confusion was matched by Angie's, who said, "Pamela Tiffin what?"

"When we were out the other night, you said Sandi reminded you of an actress from some old movie. I don't know what the movie was that you were thinking of, but the actress had to be Pamela Tiffin. Sandi could be her sister."

"Really?" Sandi asked.

"Really! She was in a bunch of movies in the '60s. The only two I can remember the names of are *Harper* and *For Those Who Think Young*."

"That last one's the one. About surfers?"

"That's it." She laughed. "And you are not going to believe it when I tell you the name of the character she played in the movie." She paused for dramatic effect and was rewarded by two sets of anxious eyes.

"Sandy, with a 'Y' instead of an 'I' but what a coincidence!"

Is she serious or kidding?

"I really look like an actress from the 1960s?"

"You can google her if you want."

Sandi gave her body a happy little shake. She never considered herself especially pretty, despite what her father kept telling her whenever he caught her crying about something, but the idea of looking like an actual Hollywood actress gave her ego an unexpected, but very welcome boost, one she sorely needed right now.

"So, would you like to stand around the foyer for a while longer, or should we go get comfortable and I'll tell you a little about myself and how I think I can help you conquer the clumsies?"

When they settled into the comfortable living room furniture, Jessica began her story.

"I grew up tripping over my own feet and dropping or

knocking over everything I touched. Does that sound familiar?"

She was staring at Sandi, who nodded.

"I thought so. When you were young, were your mom and maybe your teachers always telling you to stand up straight?"

Again Sandi nodded.

"Do you get lost easily? Have trouble following complex directions? Maybe have trouble with reading and handwriting?"

"Yes to everything but the reading. How do you know all this?"

"Because you and I have something called dyspraxia. A part of our brains didn't develop normally. You can google that, too, later if you want to read up on it. There are all kinds of professional therapies for all the various manifestations of the condition, but I literally stumbled on something when I was fourteen and it changed my life.

"I was in the library one day doing research for a report on Brazil when I heard someone say my name and I turned and knocked over a book display. As you can imagine, the whole library started to laugh, or at least the kids did. The librarians weren't too happy but it wasn't my first disaster there and I think they felt sorry for me. One of them came and helped me right the stand and put all the books back.

"The very last book I picked up was on juggling. Being as clumsy as I was, I was always fascinated by jugglers. I honestly can't tell you why, but I just decided to try it and see if I could learn to juggle three oranges. Oranges were my favorite fruit back then. So I borrowed the book despite the disbelieving look I got from the librarian.

"My mother wouldn't let me play with the fruit, so I bought three beanbag balls at a joke shop and practiced every free moment for a few days, but I just couldn't get my hands in the right place more than few times in a row. So I got discouraged and gave up and forgot about the book and the balls. A week later I found them under a pile of clothes and put the book with my school bag so I could return it to the library on the way home. Then I tossed one of the balls at my trash barrel on the other side of the room and it went in! So I tossed the second one, and it missed by a few inches. But even that was amazing because normally, I'd miss by feet in random directions, not inches. The third one bounced off the rim of the trash can. I took it all as a sign.

"I got the balls and tried one last time to juggle them and I kept them going five times before I got so excited I started to shake and missed. It took me two more days to do five passes again, but I never looked back. A few weeks later, I could keep the three balls in the air for a couple of minutes."

Her hands were making juggling motions as she spoke. She met Sandi's eyes and smiled. "Can you imagine how it felt to be able to do that?"

"Oh, yes! It must have been wonderful, especially at that age."

"It was. But it was nothing compared to what I felt a couple of months later when we were eating supper. My mother watched me the whole time with this odd look in her eyes. It was making me nervous. So finally I just said, 'What?! Why do you keep staring at me?'

"She looked at my brother, then at my father, and then back at me and said, 'Because it just occurred to me that you haven't dropped or knocked over anything at the table all week. Perhaps longer.'

"I realized she was right. I hadn't. I was so filled with joy I jumped up to run around the table to hug her and promptly tripped and fell. But I didn't care. I'd gotten my hands under control and nothing was going to make me feel bad that night.

"Mom and my brother knew I'd been juggling, but my dad had no idea. So when I started talking about it, I noticed his thinking look in his eyes. And as we were eating dessert, he suggested that, since practicing juggling with my hands brought *them* under control, maybe dance lessons would do the same for my feet. And they did. And that's the story of how I beat most of my dyspraxia. And it's how I ended up doing parties for children once I realized people would pay me to juggle and dance and make kids laugh."

Sandi's expression was a mixture of amazement, disbelief, and hope. "Are you telling me that if I learn to juggle and dance I won't be a klutz anymore?"

"I'm saying it worked for me and if you're willing to practice until your arms and legs are ready to fall off, it might do the same for you." She grinned. "Well, maybe not 'till they're ready to fall off."

Since Sandi was unemployed and Jessica's work was virtually all late-afternoons, evenings, and weekends, they decided the lessons would be Monday, Wednesday, and Friday mornings with Sandi practicing at home the other days. Jessica showed her how to hold and catch, then gave her a set of three beanbag balls.

"Alternate hands, tossing one up a little and catching it with the same hand. You don't have to throw it high. You just want to get used to the feel of tossing it and catching it. Once you're comfortable tossing and catching, start tossing them a little higher. Try to focus on something straight ahead of you, not on your hands, when you try to catch it. Just try to put your hand where you think it will come down. When you can toss and catch ten in a row, toss it higher. As you toss it higher and higher, you'll start missing more. It's normal so don't get discouraged. And don't try to use more than one."

~ ~ ~

After Angie dropped her off, Sandi practiced for hours and then for more hours Sunday. At first, it was easy, but as Jessica predicted, when she started tossing it higher, she began missing a lot more than she caught. Frustration was building when her mother walked by her room and stopped to watch for a minute.

"It looks to me like your hand is going back to about the same place after you throw it up, but when you throw it up, it doesn't go straight. Maybe it would help to practice just moving your hand straight up and down for awhile."

"But that's what I'm trying to do."

"I know, honey but...do you remember that old movie we watched a few years ago called *The Karate Kid*?"

"Where the old guy teaches the kid karate and gives him that cool old yellow car?"

"That's the one. Remember how he made the kid do things like wash cars and sand a deck and paint?"

"Riiight." Sandi alternated circular motions with her hands as she said, "Wax on, wax off."

"The one I'm thinking of is 'paint the fence' where he had to use straight up and down movements. Maybe you should try something like that."

"But how do I keep it straight?" she muttered as her mother left. Sandy sat on her bed and stared at the picture of Matt Damon that occupied her wall since she was twelve. Then she closed her eyes and imagined him as Jason Bourne sitting next to her, trying to help her find a solution to her problem, but her thoughts quickly shifted from him helping her to her helping herself to him. Her eyes snapped open as she sighed, "If only you weren't just a picture on the wall."

That's when it hit her. "The wall! Thank you, Matt!" She jumped up and did something she had not done for many years. She leaned over her desk and kissed his picture smack on the lips.

She moved her clothes hamper, stood next to the wall and brought her hand up into the throwing position, her thumb just touching it. Then she closed her eyes and began the tossing and return motions, always keeping her hand brushing the wall. After awhile, she tried it with the beanbag. Her tosses were better, but some still either hit the wall or went forward or to the side.

Well over an hour later, she realized that when her mind wandered back to Jason Bourne or off to something else, she seemed to do better than when she concentrated on the throwing. So as she turned around to practice with the other hand, Jason joined her on an adventure that ended where she always dreamed to be, in his arms.

~ ~ ~

"You're doing very well," Jessica told her. "Is it all the practice or has Jason Bourne inspired you?"

Sandi giggled. "Some of both, I think."

"Are you finding you're less clumsy with your hands?"

"A little, maybe. But it's only been three weeks."

"True. Show me how you're doing juggling two with one hand."

Sandi grabbed two balls with her right hand and tossed one in the air. When it reached the top of its arc, she tossed the second, caught the first, and kept them going for a minute. Then she arced one, then the other to the side and continued the routine with her left hand.

"Wow! That wasn't part of your homework! You figured that out on your own?"

Sandi beamed with pride. "I just combined the single arc transfer with the two-in-one. It took me a whole day to get it right."

"Well, if you can do that, maybe it's time to try the three-ball cascade. Watch me"

Jessica showed her the starting position and the throws and catches that kept two balls in the air at all times. Then she watched Sandi try and fail repeatedly for half-an-hour.

"This is so different, having to think about where both hands are every second."

"Then stop thinking about them. You know how to toss one ball from your right to your left and back again. That's really all you're doing here once you get the three of them going. Trust your hands."

So she did, and over the next half hour she did better and better until Jessica called for a break.

"Have you been looking for a job?" Jessica asked, once they were settled at her kitchen table with glasses of flavored water.

"No. Well, I did in the beginning, but when my dad found out what I was doing with the juggling, he told me not to worry about working, that he'd give me money when I needed it if I really concentrated on practicing. So I've been practicing all day most days, like it *was* a job."

"Gee, you have a great father."

"I know. I think he looks at it as an investment so I won't end up living with them for the rest of my life."

They shared a laugh that was interrupted by the doorbell. A few seconds later, Sandi heard, "Ryan! What are you doing here? Why aren't you in school?"

"Classes were cancelled. There's some kind of demonstration happening on campus and to tell the truth, even if they hadn't cancelled, I'd have cut out anyway. I work too hard to earn my tuition to waste time screaming about ducks or politicians or whatever the outrage of the day is."

"Well, don't stand there. Come in."

Seconds later, Jessica returned followed by a tall, slim guy who wasn't Jason Bourne, but who sent a Bourne-like quiver through Sandi's stomach nevertheless.

"Sandi, this is my brother Ryan Catalano. Ryan, this is my friend Sandi Sayman."

"Pleased to meet you," they said in unison and then, together, laughed.

"Why have I never met you before?" he asked, his gaze sweeping from head to toe and back again.

"You know Barry and Angie. Sandi is their friend Trane's sister. She's learning to juggle."

"An apprentice?"

"No, just learning to juggle."

"I'm sorry if I interrupted your lesson," he said to Sandi.

"That's okay. We were taking a break."

"Sit down," Jessica said. "Are you still mainlining orange juice?"

He answered with a grin and a nod.

She took a bottle from the fridge, fetched a glass, and slid back into her seat.

They talked and joked for nearly half-an-hour. Sandi found she had difficulty keeping her mind on the conversation with such a cute guy around. Finally, Jessica said it was time to get back to work.

"I guess I should go then?" Ryan asked.

Jessica's eyes questioned Sandi who said, "I don't mind if he stays and watches. I've never done it with an audience." She turned to Ryan. "But you have to promise not to laugh. I'm not very good yet."

"I never laugh at pretty girls unless they tell a joke."

He thinks I'm pretty!

"Okay then."

Back in the large family room, Ryan flopped onto the

sofa while Sandi did a little warm up. Then she did the two-in-one, switching hands several times. When she ended the routine, Ryan applauded, which brought some color to her cheeks.

"That was great. I thought you said you were just learning?"

"I am. Wait 'till you see what happens next."

Sandi turned partly away from him, knowing that if she could see him, it would be too distracting. With three balls in hand, she tried the cascade. Plop. The first ball hit the floor. As she picked it up, she felt her face growing warm. Then she remembered what Jessica said about trusting her hands. So she did, and made six tosses before dropping one. Twenty minutes later, she was averaging ten tosses before a drop.

"You are doing really well," Jessica said. "Just keep working on that over the weekend until you can keep them going for five minutes. If you get that far, see if you can get your mom or someone to talk with you while you juggle."

"I will, thanks." She glanced at her watch. "I have to go so I don't miss the eleven-thirty bus."

"You take the bus here?" Ryan asked. "From where?"

"The city. West End"

His brow furrowed. "That must take forty-five minutes."

"Usually about fifty. But I'm used to the bus."

"Ah. No car."

He turned to his sister. "I stopped by to see if you want to go visit Grams with me. The West End won't be much out of the way. We can give Sandi a ride home."

"Damn! I'd really like to see Grammy, but I have a gig at a school fair this afternoon. But go without me. She'll be thrilled to see you. And drop Sandi off on the way."

Sandi buckled her seat belt before taking a few sniffs and wrinkling her nose.

God, is this how he always smells?

She watched him walk around the front of the car to the driver's door.

As soon as he got in, he, too, sniffed and said, "I'm sorry. I thought I'd aired the car out enough before I got here. I stopped at Andleman's this morning and a very lovely young lady asked me to sample a new scent they were selling. It's called *Deep Woodsman*." He pulled a folded postcard from his visor. "I'm supposed to have my wife or girlfriend give her opinion about it, but since I have neither, would you care to provide a feminine opinion of this 'manly new scent'? It's supposed to remind you of a romantic walk in the forest. Does it do that for you?"

"Uhh…not exactly."

"More like walking in the forest and stepping in a bear turd, maybe?"

Sandi giggled and nodded.

He started the car and rolled down all the windows. "I'm guessing you won't mind some fresh air as we drive. I wiped the stuff off my wrist with one of those hand-wash things, but the smell seems to have insinuated itself into the upholstery."

"That's okay. You should smell some of the stuff they try to sell women."

"I have." He backed out of the driveway and started down the street. "A couple of years ago I went out with this girl who was addicted to perfumes. Every time we went out she smelled different and most of them were pretty bad. I kept trying to tell her that she didn't need all that junk but advertisers had more influence than I did. It's too bad, too. I kind of liked her but I just could not deal with the merry-go-round of awful smells. Are you a perfume person?"

"Not really."

"Good. Soaps and shampoos have all the scents anyone needs, man or woman. At least *I* think so. So, no car? Are you another victim of the quote economic downturn unquote?"

"No, not really. I've never driven a car. I can't."

"It's really not that hard. I could teach you if you like."

"I know it's…it's not…"

Just tell him. What does it matter?

"You know the condition Jess has?"

"Dys-something or other?"

"Dyspraxia. I have it too. I'm so uncoordinated I'd probably kill someone or myself if I tried to drive a car."

She explained how she came to be taking juggling lessons and how she noticed a real improvement in her clumsiness since she began.

"That's great! It must make you *feel* great."

"It does. For the first time ever, I've began to feel hope that someday I'll be normal."

As they drove, he regaled her with funny stories about famous spills, drops, and trips in the Catalano house when he and Jessica were children. By the time she said goodbye, she was feeling happier than she could ever remember just from learning she really wasn't a freak after all, that someone else had suffered the same embarrassments and humiliations growing up and that someday soon, it might all be over.

~ ~ ~

By Friday of week seven, not only was Sandi proficient in several three-ball routines, she was well on her way to mastering four balls. In addition, she and Jessica were working on simple two-person numbers, which presented a very different challenge. But for Sandi, the most exciting thing of all was her first week without a single hand-caused accident.

"I'm so happy for you!" Jessica said when Sandi released her from the 'thank you' hug. "You know, you are doing so well, I think it might be time to cut down on the juggling practice."

"No! I love to practice. I feel so good when I nail something new."

"I know, but had you let me finish, I was going to say it's time we begin working on your feet and body motion."

"Dancing?"

"We have to start sometime."

"But I've never been able to dance. I can jump around on the floor, but following someone or doing a line dance or…"

"Relax. We're going to start with very easy steps, the equivalent of tossing the ball a few inches in the air. I'll lead, you follow. And even if you mess up, you're nowhere near heavy enough to hurt my toes."

Sandi's worried frown became a grin. "Okay. They're your feet."

~ ~ ~

Yesterday, despite the simplicity of the box step, Sandi spent a frustrating morning with Jessica. She was fine when they paused between each step, but whenever Jessica tried to string them together, Sandi's steps would be too short or too long or end up on her partner's foot. On the bus ride home, she decided she would do nothing else over the weekend except practice the steps until she could do them without thinking.

On the wall in front of her was a diagram of the steps. Under her feet, blue painter's tape formed Xs on the floor at spots corresponding to the diagram. And she had her game face on.

Backward, diagonal, side, forward, diagonal, side. Backward, diagonal, side, forward, diagonal, side.

The steps were burned into her brain, but her feet didn't always listen. Nevertheless, she was determined and kept at it. After the second hour, her feet were finding the marks most of the time, so she decided to take a break. She wanted to practice ending the three-ball cascade with a catch behind her back so that one day soon, she could surprise Jessica again.

She was not sure if it was because Jessica was a new friend, or because she was her teacher, or because she admired the woman and what she achieved despite her condition, but Sandi found herself craving her approval and almost impatiently looking forward to their thrice-weekly sessions. The elation engendered by Jessica's smiles and nods, her words of praise, reminded Sandi of her childhood, when nearly everything she did was with the goal of making her mother or father smile and nod and tell her how good she was. But it all began to ring hollow as she grew and began to compare what she could do to the talents of her friends and classmates.

A memory surfaced of the day when, as she sat on the swing in the backyard, she realized her parents had been lying to her. Her voice wasn't that of an angel but closer to a banshee. Her amazing two-left-foot dances were just clown routines, complete with unplanned pratfalls.

As it so often does, the truth hurt, and her tears were still falling when her brother found her sometime later. In very un-older-brotherly-like fashion, he got her to tell him why she was crying, then explained mom and dad lied because they loved her so much and couldn't bear to see her hurt or unhappy. He likened it to their letting her win at *Candy Land* and other games when she was a little girl. By the time their mother called them for supper, she was again smiling. She even changed her mind about all brothers being stupid-brains until, a few days later, he refused to let her hang out with him and his friends when she really, really wanted to.

Sandi retrieved the balls from the top of her dresser and warmed up, keeping the balls going for several minutes before she ended by catching two and trying to toss the last ball high and just behind her. It hit her on the head. The next one hit her shoulder. The third landed two feet behind her. Then she had an idea.

What if I just toss the final ball little higher and spin around to catch it. That would look a lot cooler.

She tried it a few times and found the ball hitting her arm and hand. It was an improvement, but getting her feet in the same spot each time was proving to be impossible.

Maybe I should save this until after I have more dance lessons.

She returned the balls to the dresser and resumed practicing the box step until her mother called her for lunch.

~ ~ ~

"Oh my god! What happened to you?"

When Sandi arrived at Jessica's house Monday morning, she found her on crutches with her left foot in a cast.

"Remember I had a show Friday afternoon? Well it was going great until the part where I toss a ball up and behind me, do a back-flip and catch it, do another back-flip, toss it, etc. Halfway through the series, some kid knocks a ball out of another kid's hand and it rolls right into my landing spot. I was upside down in the air when I saw it and tried to twist away from it but my foot caught the side of the ball. I landed hard and crooked and I ended up with two cracked bones. So I'm out of commission for the next two months plus whatever time it takes me to rehab and strengthen the foot and leg and get myself sharp again."

"That's awful! I feel so bad for you. Want me to find that stupid kid and smack him for you?"

That lightened Jessica's mood a little. "Nah, you'd probably just get arrested. And then how would you practice?"

"I don't know. But it might be worth it to teach the little brat a lesson." They shared a laugh. "Oh well, I guess I'll just keep practicing at my house until you're well again."

"Nonsense. I may not be able to do much, but there's no reason for that to hold you back. I can keep teaching you."

"Seriously? All right! I'll just concentrate on the juggling and forget the dancing for now."

"Speaking of which, how did that go over the weekend?"

She explained how she practiced and by Sunday afternoon wasn't missing a step. Then she asked her mother to try it with her and tried to lead and totally flubbed it.

"I could follow pretty well, but starting with my other foot in another direction threw everything off!" A sadness came over her. "She looked so proud of me when I was doing the steps on the markers, going faster and faster and not missing even one." She sighed. "Oh well."

"Hey, cheer up. You did great with your homework. And if this hadn't happened, you'd be practicing leading with me today. Which reminds me. Do you have to leave as you usually do or can you hang around and keep me company?"

"Really? I'd love to stay and hang out with you. Can I practice, too, some of the time?"

Jessica laughed. "Of course. You really are into this,

aren't you?"

Sandi's head bobbed up and down. "I love it. I never thought I'd ever be anything but a klutz my whole life and you changed everything. Everything above the waist, that is, so far. And in a few months, we'll be able to start on my legs and feet and…and…" She choked up and felt her eyes tearing as she hurried to where Jessica was sitting, fell to her knees, and hugged her. "Thank you so much," she sniffled. "I don't know how I can ever repay you for what you're doing for me."

The two had a wonderful day, alternating juggling instruction and practice with goofing, girl-talk, and laughing at daytime TV, bringing them even closer than they had become prior to Jessica's accident.

"Will you stay for dinner?" Jessica asked, noting the time was approaching four o'clock.

"Aren't you tired of me yet?"

"Are you kidding? I haven't had this much fun since…well, I don't know when. I'm almost always on the go, doing something, and this sitting with my leg up got real tired by last night. I was dreading today and the next six to eight weeks. But I had a great time today. As far as I'm concerned, you can hang out here whenever you want to and I hope you will, at least on our practice days. So, supper?"

It had been a very long time since Sandi, too, enjoyed a day as much as she did today and the thought of repeating it three times a week for the next few months made her feel so giddy she had to struggle not to gush her pleasure.

"I'd love to stay for supper. But only if you let me cook."

"Cook? Uh-uh. Zack's bringing home Thai tonight." She picked up her phone. "I'll tell him to order enough for three." Just then, the doorbell rang. "Or four. Would you get that while I call."

She hurried to the front door and pulled it open. "Ryan!"

"Sandi!" he said, aping her surprised tone. "I'm glad to see you're still here."

"You knew I was staying all day?"

"I knew you might be," he said as they joined Jessica. "Are you ready for your lesson?"

Sandi was confused. "I've already had juggling lessons today."

He looked at his sister. "You didn't tell her."

"No. I thought I'd let it be a surprise."

"Surprise? What surprise? I love surprises!"

"Jess called me yesterday. She didn't want you to have to wait for months to continue your dance lessons so she asked me to take over for her until she can move around again."

Sandi looked from Ryan to Jessica, who nodded, back to Ryan. "You know how to dance?"

His laughter made her blush. "Just a little. I teach dance part-time at Childer Dance Studios. I normally work weekday evenings from five to eight. If you want, you could come at four. There are classes in the ballroom but there's small studio we can use. And you wouldn't have to come all the way out here. Heck, I could even pick you up at your house since it's just as easy to go by there on the way to the studio."

"You're really a dance teacher?"

I guess that explains slim and muscular.

"Would you like a demonstration? Jess said she showed you a simple box step last week. Did you practice it?"

"All weekend."

He walked over to the stereo, selected a CD and

pressed play. "Then let's dance."

Dancing with him was so different than with Jessica or her mother. For one thing, he was a guy and the way he held her and led her felt different, even though the steps were the same. She found herself resisting the urge to move closer to him, which distracted her enough to make her misstep and land a foot on his toe. But he just paused, reassured her she was doing fine, and picked up the rhythm again.

When the song was over, he told her they were going to use the same one-two-three rhythm for a slow waltz. Instead of simply moving over and over in a rectangle, they'd be turning. They practiced for a few minutes while Jessica watched and nodded her encouragement, then he restarted the music and they began dancing. But while her body had no trouble being led in gentle turns, her feet couldn't manage to keep up. She felt herself burning with embarrassment each time she stumbled or stepped on his foot and felt herself on the verge of tears when he stopped.

"I'm sorry about that," he said. "but I wanted to see how your body and feet would react to the change. I think the dyspraxia affects your foot coordination more than it did Jessie."

He turned to his sister, who agreed, and asked Sandi, "How long did you say you practiced before you were hitting the steps continuously?"

"Friday, Saturday, and part of Sunday."

Ryan let out a thoughtful, "Hmmm." followed by, "Here's the thing. I'm not sure practicing on your own is going to work with dancing the way it did with juggling. Juggling works as a solitary exercise, but dancing, at least ballroom dancing, is different. Not only do your feet have to coordinate with the rest of your body, they have to coordinate with your partner's feet and body.

"Monday, Tuesday, and Thursday, my classes are over by three. Wednesday and Friday I'm out at two-thirty. How about I pick you up at your house after school each day and we'll go to the studio and practice until my first lesson?"

"I can't ask you to give up hours every day just to help me."

"You didn't ask. I'm offering."

"And I already told Jess I'd hang out with her here on lesson days until she recovered."

"Okay, then how about on Tuesday and Thursday, I pick you up at your house and on the other days I pick you up here."

Sandi still looked skeptical. She didn't understand why he'd give up ten or fifteen hours a week for months just to teach her to dance.

As if he had read her mind, he said, "Look, Jessie told me what amazing progress you've made with the juggling. She also told me she felt like you two were becoming real friends, and she *is* my sister and I love her." He faked gagging, then stage whispered, "And she really doesn't have any friends. People just let her hang around because Zack is such a cool guy."

Jessica bounced one of her small beanbag balls off the back of his head as she laughed. "You really *are* a jerk, Ryan." She turned to Sandi. "Is your brother this big of a jerk?"

"He's older than me, but there *have* been times when I wanted to hit him with something a lot harder than a beanbag ball."

"Okay," Ryan said. "Before this man-bashing escalates, I really do want to help you do as well with dancing as you've done with juggling. Better, even. I may have been a few years younger than Jessie when she beat the dyspraxia, but what she accomplished wasn't lost on me." He glanced her way for a second. "It was inspiring. I didn't take up juggling, but she's the reason I started dancing." He resorted to the stage whisper again. "Don't tell her because her ego is big enough already, but she's always kind of been my hero." Serious replaced fun on his face. "And she's always been there for me and helped me whenever I needed it, and now I have a chance to do something for her in return.

"If she thinks you're ready to start integrating dance with the juggling, then you shouldn't have to wait. And while Jessie is good at dancing…" His face broke into a grin as he did few quick steps that ended with a twirl and a flourish. "…*I* am a professional! Besides, most of my dancing these days is done with middle-aged women. Dancing with someone as pretty as you will be a refreshing change."

~ ~ ~

Sandi stood at the window, thinking, waiting for Ryan's car to appear.

Yesterday, after working with her for a bit longer, Ryan stayed for dinner, then gave her a ride home. All the while, his words echoed in her head as they continued to do now.

Dancing with someone as pretty as you will be a refreshing change.

She knew he was just trying to be funny when he said it, but no cute guy had ever given her the time of day before, much less said she was pretty while offering to help her the way he had. She silently chastised herself for being silly.

This is a great opportunity and if I start obsessing over a chance comment I'll get distracted and not be able to concentrate on the dancing and then he'll give up and then where will I be? Right where I am now. And Jess will be disappointed and probably not want to be my friend anymore and I really like her. So just forget about it and concentrate on learning to dance.

She did just that. On the short ride to the studio, they made small talk. When he stood next to her, showing her how to move her feet, or demonstrated the steps, first slowly, then at normal speed, she focused on his feet. And when he took her hand in his and placed the other at her waist, she concentrated her mind on the steps and her eyes on the tip of his nose instead of his bright hazel eyes flecked with gold.

For his part, as the weeks passed, Ryan was always a perfect gentleman and teacher, mixing humor, enthusiasm, and lots of positive feedback into the lessons and practice. Never once did he flirt or raise so much as a suggestive eyebrow so, while Sandi still treasured his remark that day, she accepted it for what it was, kept her concentration, and made steady progress.

~ ~ ~

Jessica's cast was shed permanently after seven weeks. Thanks to the twice-weekly home physical therapy her doctor ordered, she was soon able to walk with reasonable comfort and even start driving again. And after three more weeks of thrice-weekly therapy at the outpatient clinic in the city, she felt as good as new.

"But he said no extra stress on the foot for at least two more months, so I can't jump or tumble or do flips. Half my act is out."

"That stinks," Sandi said. "But can't you just do juggling routines that don't involve any of that?"

"I could, but the act wouldn't be the same. And you know how it is. Even when you're doing something simple, sometimes you need to make a quick, unplanned movement. It's only another couple of months and I really don't want to risk anything that might make it longer before I can get back to work. I really miss the kids." She sighed. "So how's the dancing coming along?"

Sandi's face lit up. "Ryan said I'm now, quote, proficient, unquote in the box step, waltz, and foxtrot and I'm doing well with the quickstep. He's even teaching me the two-step and some line dances."

"That's great!"

"I know. And I hardly ever trip anymore. He wants me to start learning dances like the tango and cha cha and samba but first..." Her eyes widened as her face scrunched. "...he says I have to learn to dance in heels, since women are always in heels at weddings and functions where there's ballroom dancing. God, I hope he has steel-toed dancing shoes!"

~ ~ ~

"What's in the bag?" Ryan asked as he pulled away from the curb.

"My shoes. I bought some comfortable heels so we can practice dancing in them."

He slowed and stopped as the traffic light changed. "Can I see them?"

He examined the shoes for a few seconds before asking, "Can you return them?"

"Why? What's wrong with them?"

"There's nothing wrong. They look like nice shoes. But they're too stiff and certainly not constructed for dancing. If you step wrong, which will probably happen in the beginning, you could roll an ankle or the heel could break off. We're going shoe-shopping today to get you a professional pair. Then we'll stop at a cobbler who will reinforce the shank and heel for stability and so the heel won't break. That will take a couple of days, so we won't actually start with you dancing in heels until Thursday or Friday."

"Uhh...what is this all going to cost?"

"Depending on the shoes you pick, probably a

hundred-thirty to a hundred fifty dollars."

"Ryan, I don't have that much money and I can't ask my father to spend that much on shoes for me."

"Oh. Right. I didn't think of that. Well, don't worry, I'll…"

"No!"

"No what?"

"You were going to offer to pay for them and I can't let you do that. It's not right. You're already doing so much for me and I really appreciate it, but I can't take money from you. Or shoes."

"Hmmm. Well, I appreciate all the time you've spent keeping Jessie company so why don't we consider it…"

"No. I'm not taking money for hanging out with my friend."

"Hmm, hmm, hmm."

He pulled into a parking lot and took out his cell phone. "Hi, sis. I have a bit of a problem and I need your help."

He replayed the shoe saga for her, then listened, muttering only the occasional "uh-ha" before finally saying, "Got it. See you later. And thanks."

He shifted in his seat to face her. "Jessie says that for the past several months you have indeed been keeping her company after the juggling lessons and that she thinks of you as a very good friend."

"See. I can't…"

"Let me finish, please. She also said that during that time, you helped clean the house, did laundry for her, cooked, and made it so she could follow doctor's orders and just sit or lie down with her foot elevated most of the time. Is all that true?"

"Yeesss."

"Well, if you had not done all that for her, she would have had to hire a housekeeper or figured out how to get

Zack to do it to her standards, a virtual impossibility. So she told me to tell you that you are perfectly correct not to take money from me, but that you better let her buy you the shoes as a thank-you gift or her feelings are going to be very, very hurt."

Knowing she was beat, Sandi nodded and smiled. "I swear, I have never met anyone nicer than you and Jess."

"Well, we've grown kind of fond of you, too."

~ ~ ~

Sandi kicked off her shoes and slid her feet into her new dancing heels. When they went shopping, she fell in love with a pair of black, strappy 4-inch heels but Ryan insisted that for safety sake, she limit the heel to two-and-a-half inches. The pair she selected not only looked beautiful on her feet, but the extra padding and reinforcement made them the most comfortable heels she ever wore. Not that she wore heels very often, given her former tendency to tip over.

Although she barely wobbled at first in the shoe store, it was the memory of too many embarrassing moments that knotted her stomach as she fastened the straps and stood up.

They began simply, by strolling around the room, alternately walking forward and backward, until Sandi felt the shoes were an extension of her feet. Then they traversed the room with side steps several times, going all the way right, then left, back to where they began. Finally, he led her to the center of the room, twirled her once, which she executed perfectly on the balls of her feet, and they began at the beginning again, with the simple box step.

~ ~ ~

By the following Friday, it was clear her feet knew what to do to compensate for the heels. She was so accustomed to the waltz embrace and being held closer for a foxtrot, that she followed Ryan's lead effortlessly. She was even doing well with the tango and cha cha. When their time was up for the day, he sat down next to her as she changed back into street shoes.

"I have a surprise for you. I hope you'll like it. I wasn't sure it was a good idea, which is why I put you through so much today. But you did fantastic."

"Thanks! You make it easy to follow your lead. So what's the surprise?"

"Jess and Zack are going out tomorrow night with Barry and Angie. Going to a dinner and dance club and I thought we might go with them, to see if you do as well in public as you do here in private. And you'll get to dance with two other guys. What do you think? Are you up for it? And no arguments, it will be my treat."

Her old insecurities welled up from wherever they had been hiding for the past months. "You want me to dance in public? Like with lots of other people on the dance floor and people watching me? But what if I…I mean…"

Ryan saw the panic in her eyes. He slid his chair next to hers and put his arm across her shoulders. "Sandi, if you don't want to go that's okay. But I wouldn't have suggested it if I didn't think you could do it. Besides, even if we don't dance much, the food is pretty good there and it will be fun hanging out with them."

"You really think I can do it?"

"I know you can. I mean it. Now go home, pick out a nice dress to wear, and don't forget to wear your dancing shoes. I'll pick you up at seven-thirty sharp."

On the bus, Sandi's anxiety fluctuated between dancing in public and what she would wear. Once home, she dashed to her room and jumped on the club's website. The photos showed people of all ages, all dressed in evening or party clothes.

She was in the process of tearing her closet apart, desperately trying to figure out what she had that would not brand her as a no-style loser, when she heard her mother ask, "What in the world are you looking for?"

She slumped to the floor and explained.

"Ryan asked you on a date?"

"No, mom. It's not a date. I told you. It's just a test, I guess, to see how I do in public."

"Well, dinner and dancing certainly constituted a date when I was your age. But never mind. Let's see if we can find something."

Ten minutes later it was clear Sandi owned nothing that would pass muster as evening wear. Her mother pursed her lips, shook her head, and said, "Put all this stuff back in the closet. I'll be back in a few minutes."

She was only half done when her mother returned. "Leave the rest for later. Come on. I told your father you and I are going shopping."

When her mother pulled into the parking lot of the boutique, Sandi's head snapped around to see if she looked lost. "We're going here? This place is kind of expensive. Dad will have a fit if we buy something here."

Her mother laid her hand on Sandi's cheek. "Ever since you started walking, and falling, I've prayed for a miracle like this. You've always been my beautiful little flower and it broke my heart to see you struggle, to see kids make fun of you, to hear you crying because boys never called. But these past months, I've watched you bloom, becoming more poised and confident by the day. Don't you worry about your father. I'll take care of him. It's about damn time my baby had some clothes that will knock the boys' socks off."

Most of Sandi's wardrobe consisted of jeans and

pants and tops because pants never flew up or bunched around your waist when you fell, adding humiliation to embarrassment. Only rarely did she wear a dress and when she did, they were long to lessen the chance of anything showing that shouldn't. But today, her mother steered her away from evening gowns to the cocktail dresses.

She tried on dress after dress, but even the ones she thought looked okay received head-shakes from her mother. After the ninth rejection, her mother handed her a black, v-neck, pleated dress and asked her to try it on.

"But it's sleeveless! And backless! I'll be half naked in this."

"Don't be ridiculous. Of course you won't. Just go try it on."

When she emerged from the changing room two minutes later she said, "I can't wear this. My bra is showing in the front and the back."

Her mother sighed. "Go back in and take off your bra."

"What! But…"

"Sandi, just do it, please. Humor me. And stand up straight when you come out."

Shaking her head, she did as requested, and when she walked back through the door again, she saw her mother's hand fly to her mouth as tears filled her eyes.

"Oh my." She hurried forward, put her hands on Sandi's shoulders and turned her. "Look in the mirror. See how beautiful you look."

She did. When she saw herself in the dress, she almost couldn't believe it *was* her. The wide, beaded belt cinched the flowing fabric so the hem floated just above her knees. And the neck plunged low enough to show a hint of cleavage.

I look beautiful!

When she lifted her eyes to her face, she saw it was glowing. Then she did a couple of quick dance steps and the glow vanished.

Her mother noticed and asked, "What wrong, sweetie?"

"Mom, I can't dance in this. My boobs will go flying all over the place. I need a dress so I can wear a bra."

If Sandi had not been so focused on imagining her breasts being exposed while she danced, she might have noticed the look of amusement and guilt that inhabited her mother's face and might have guessed her thoughts.

Good Lord forgive me. How did I let my sweet girl get to this age so unprepared to be a woman?

"You still wear a 34-B, right?"

Sandi nodded, still lost in her distressing daydream.

"Stay there. I'll be back in a few minutes."

When she returned, she handed her daughter a package. "You'll need someone to show you how to put this on the first time. Do you want me or the salesgirl to help?"

"What is it?"

"A quarter-cup, backless, strapless bra."

"What? How can…"

"You'll see. It sticks. Me or the salesgirl?"

"You, of course. Sticks?"

A few minutes later, her mother stepped back and said, "See. Just like magic. It pushes you up and together. Now get the top back in place and come see how nice you're going to look."

When she stepped in front of the mirror again, Sandi's eyes became saucers of disbelief. Not only did she still look beautiful, she looked sexy!

I look hot!

She caught the beaming pride in her mother's reflection. But still…her hand went to her chest.

"Ma, I can't go out in public like this. Half my boobs are showing. Daddy will disown me if he sees me dressed like this."

"Don't exaggerate. Half your chest is not showing. It's just a little cleavage. And the right amount of cleavage catches a man's eye without sending the wrong message."

"Mom! I can't believe you said that!"

"Ha! You think I wasn't young once? You think I never showed a little cleavage? How do you think I caught your father?"

"Eewww!" Her face scrunched in distaste at being made to imagine her parents as sexual beings, but then softened. "You really dressed like this when you were my age?"

Her mother laughed. "Sweetie, when I was your age, the material it took to make what you're wearing would have made two dresses. When we get home, remind me to get out the picture albums of when I was young. And be prepared for a shock because the boys back then all thought your mom was one shagadelic chick!"

~ ~ ~

"Mom! It's almost seven-thirty. He'll be here any minute."

Sandi never wore makeup, but her mother insisted that going to a fancy club required at least a little.

"So he'll wait a few minutes. It does men good to wait for their dates. Teaches them patience and that good things are worth waiting for. Now keep still."

"Mom, I keep telling you this isn't a date."

"Whether it is or isn't, you should look your best. If he's not interested in you there may be other boys there who will be."

It never occurred to Sandi that her newfound coordination might result in guys showing interest. But as her mother put the finishing touches on her face, she imagined dancing with Ryan a few times and then other guys coming over to ask her to dance. The prospect excited her, but she cautioned herself to stay calm and relaxed, lest her inner klutz find an opening to assert itself.

A knock on the door received a "Come in."

Trane stuck his head in and said, "Hey, brat, you look great. And Ryan is downstairs waiting for you."

"He came in? He was supposed to call when he got here."

"Yeah, he said that, but he figured you wouldn't be ready anyway so he might as well wait inside instead of in his car. He seems pretty cool. He's in the living room with dad, who's probably grilling him as we speak."

"Oh, god! Mom!"

"Relax. I'll go down now and take care of your father. Don't forget your purse, you look lovely and will fit right in there. And have a wonderful time."

Trane and her mother left her alone to make sure her purse contained all the items she might need for the evening. Then she took a final look in the mirror, settled on a smile, and headed for the stairs.

When she reached the bottom, she heard Trane and Ryan talking about baseball. And when she reached the archway to the living room, she was happy to see her mother had, indeed, taken care of her father. She stood there, waiting for one of the guys to notice her. Trane did, and smiled.

Ryan saw the smile, glanced over, and did a double take. His mouth fell open as he rose. "Oh, wow. You look fantastic!"

His eyes widened to let in more of the vision and Sandi felt an unfamiliar flutter at the obvious admiration. She turned to Trane and said, "Tell Mom and Dad goodbye for me?" Then to Ryan, "Shall we go?"

Sandi felt a different vibe from Ryan as he drove to the club. He was quieter, more reserved, and by the time they were halfway there, had not joked one time. Finally, she asked, "Is something wrong? Am I dressed wrong for this club?"

"No. No. Nothing's wrong. Your dress is…" He drew a deep breath. "You really do look amazing. It's just that, well, I've grown used to you in jeans and shirts and, you know, dressed down, and seeing you all dressed to kill sort of startled me. I guess I'm a little embarrassed to realize I never noticed what a beautiful woman you really are."

His squished face forced his eyes into a squint, as if he wasn't sure what reaction to expect from his confession.

"You really think I'm beautiful?"

He released the breath he was holding. "Are you kidding? Did you look in a mirror before you came downstairs? I can hardly wait 'till Jessie and Zack get a look at you."

He didn't have to wait long. Six minutes later he turned into the club's parking lot and three minutes after that, the hostess led them to their table. When the others saw them, there was no doubt they were as startled at her appearance as Ryan had been.

Jessica hurried to meet them and said, "Sandi! My god! I can't believe how amazing you look!"

Sandi leaned in close and whispered, "Neither can I. I've never worn anything like this in my life."

"Well it suits you. And from the number of eyes turned your way, I think it suits a lot of the guys here, too."

It clearly suited Barry and Zack, who didn't even try to hide their admiration for her transformation from an ordinary girl to an extraordinary woman.

As they ate dinner, Sandi found the jitters that infected her when she and Ryan made their entrance fading. She was out in public and she was in control. Nothing was spilled or dropped or bumped despite the distractions of good food and conversation. It was, literally, a dream come true for her. The only remaining concern was the dancing. Would anxiety override all the progress she made over the past months? Would she be able to follow Ryan as smoothly in public as she learned to do in private? She was about to find out.

Ryan leaned close. "There are only a few couples on the dance floor at the moment, but after dessert, it will fill up fast. Want to take the plunge now?"

She felt her heartbeat accelerate as a swarm of butterflies invaded her stomach.

Relax, girl. You can do this.

She answered with a smile and a nod. He took her hand and led her to the dance floor, watched closely by their dinner companions, who knew the import of what was about to happen, and by a fair number of husbands, boyfriends, and companions who knew only a beautiful young woman was about to dance and all they could do was watch and wish they were up there with her.

The name of the old standard the band was playing escaped her as Ryan led her into a slow, modified box step. They moved as one around their section of the floor and by the time the song came to a close, she was radiating joy.

"That was wonderful," she said.

"*You* were wonderful," he replied, his face reinforcing the sentiment. "I knew you could do it."

Her head tilted an invitation as she recognized the opening notes of *The Sleeping Beauty Waltz*. Hands joined and settled into the proper positions. With the slightest of movements, his head nodded the 1-2-3, 1-2-3 rhythm. They began to dance but on the first step, her foot landed on his.

"Oh!"

Her cheeks burned as she froze, but Ryan kept smiling and nodding the beat and said softly, "Everyone makes mistakes, but they keep going right through them. We've waltzed a hundred times and I know you can do it. Ready?"

His confidence in her boosted her own. She nodded, they began again, and drifted across the floor in perfect synch. When her eyes sought his, they saw how proud he was of her and when she heard the final strains, she wished there was a replay button.

As the orchestra leader announced a short break, Ryan stepped back and bowed. Sandi curtsied in return, then took his arm to be escorted off the floor. They reclaimed their seats to the applause of their friends, and as they all enjoyed their mango sherbet, the two found themselves stealing glances sideways, their eyes and smiles conveying a warm admiration when the glances coincided.

An hour later, Sandi, Jessica, and Angie took their places at the end of the line in the Ladies' Room.

"I cannot believe how well you can dance," Angie gushed.

"Ryan is a very good and very patient teacher."

"Maybe so," Jessica said, "but there will be no false modesty here tonight. You've been working your legs off for months and all that practice shows. You two move together like you've been partners for years. And what was with those swing moves? I thought you only learned box, waltz, and foxtrot and started on the tango and cha cha?"

Sandi shrugged. "I don't know. When the song began I thought we'd go sit down for awhile, but he told me to stay, that he'd teach me some steps. I tried my best but I kept messing up but he told me earlier that everyone makes mistakes and to just continue on through them, so I did and had so much fun!"

"You mean a lot of that was mistakes?" Angie asked. "I thought you were improvising."

"I guess my feet were improvising and I was just along for the ride."

The eleven o'clock set was traditionally the waltz hour and the hour during which gentlemen were permitted to tap a dancer on the shoulder and cut in.

Zack and Barry were quick to take advantage, much to Ryan's chagrin. He was having a wonderful time dancing with Sandi and was loath to give up even a few steps. But he traded and danced with his sister, first, then Angie, as their husbands took turns with his star pupil for the also-traditional two minutes during which another cut-in was not allowed.

As he danced with Jessica, she confided a secret to her brother and asked his opinion. It took him aback for a few seconds, but quickly realized the sense of it and encouraged her to go for it. When he was with Angie, he found his head occupied with Sandi and her status as his student. Somehow, the label no longer felt right, but he couldn't decide why. Then he was back with her, twirling across the floor, losing himself in the motion and the loveliness he embraced until he felt a tap on his shoulder. When he returned to her, two minutes later, came another tap. Then another and it became clear there were many men who wanted to dance with Sandi that night. He nearly growled in frustration. Finally, and not a moment too soon for Ryan, the set was over.

Once back at the table, the girls again headed to the ladies' room where Sandi's popularity on the dance floor was the topic of conversation and the cause of a few untoward looks from women whose partners had abandoned them to cut in.

"How many guys did you dance with?"

"I don't know. It seemed like every time Ryan cut back in, some other guy would cut him out again. Ten, maybe more." She lowered her voice to a whisper. "One of them asked me if I wanted to go home with him and three others asked for my phone number!"

"Alright! You go girl!" Angie said. "Did you give it to them?"

"No! Of course not. I had no idea who they were. And besides, I came with Ryan. What kind of man asks a girl for her number when she's with another guy?"

Angie and Jessica shared a look, laughed and said together, "All of them."

Ryan seemed preoccupied when they returned to the table, but the musicians were taking their seats again so Sandi just asked, "If they play the right song, can we do more of that swing stuff? I had fun doing it earlier even though I know I was messing up the steps."

"Of course. You did great. There's lots of improv in swing and who's to say you messed up or tried something new?"

As they all stood and headed for the floor, Ryan said, "While you three were in the ladies room, Zack and Barry kind of insisted they get to dance with you a couple more times each. Would you mind?"

"Of course not," she said, catching his eye.

"Drats! I was hoping you'd refuse them. Oh well. I'll dance the first one with you, then we'll rotate with each new song until each guy has danced with each girl twice."

The grin that spread across his face made the gleam in his eyes brighter. "After that, you're all mine for the rest of the night."

The sentiment warmed her. Never before was she anyone's choice for anything, but thanks to Jessica and Ryan, tonight was her own, private coming out party. No longer was she a clumsy waif, little more than a source of amusement. Here, among all these people, she was a woman, a woman men found attractive and desirable. Her joy filled her to overflowing.

As she danced and danced and danced, all the disasters that once defined her, the drops and spills, the trips and falls, the laughter and humiliation, all of it was remembered and banished forever. With each step, each turn, she grew lighter and lighter, until only the new Sandi, the Sandi people liked and wanted to be with, the Sandi who Ryan wanted for himself as the night came to a close, only she remained.

When she heard the opening bars of the final song, Sandi laughed and wondered if there could possibly be any more appropriate song to end this wonderful adventure than *Cheek to Cheek*.

Ryan led her into a foxtrot while, in her head, Doris Day sang the lyrics she heard hundreds of times on the family stereo as she grew up. As they danced, Sandi felt Ryan drawing her closer and closer until her soft curves fused with his firm, muscular torso. Lifting her head, she met eyes that made her feel giddy and tingly in places where she never felt like that before, eyes that made her want to feel his lips on hers. But she knew it was just the magic of the moment, of the whole evening making her feel this way, making her want what could never really be.

All too soon, the dance was over. They moved apart, but she could still feel his warmth, and she knew it would not be Matt Damon who would visit her in her dreams tonight.

~ ~ ~

Sandi awoke to the sound of her cellphone ringing. Still half-asleep, she mumbled, "Hello?"

"Oh, you were sleeping. I'm sorry. I can call back later."

"Ryan?"

"Yeah. I really am sorry. I just…I wanted to see if I could stop by later. I need to talk with you about something."

She stifled a yawn.

What could be so important?

"Can you give me an hour to wake up and shower and get dressed?"

"Of course. I'll see you in an hour."

Ryan looked somber, almost haunted when Sandi opened the door. She led him to the living room and sat next to him on the sofa.

"What's wrong?" she asked. "You look like you've been up all night. Oh god. Did something happen to Jessie?"

"No. No. Jessie's fine. But I…I have to drop you as a student."

"Why?! Did I do something wrong? I'll stop. I'll fix it. I don't want you to stop teaching me." The alarm in her voice was unmistakable.

"Wrong?" A nervous laugh escaped. "No, you didn't do anything wrong. You've done everything right. You've been wonderful. You are wonderful. That's the problem."

"What's the problem? I don't understand."

He took a deep breath and slowly released it.

"Last night, during the waltz hour, you must have noticed I got annoyed every time someone cut in."

A nod accompanied, "Yes, I noticed. But I was annoyed, too. I like dancing with you. I mean, I didn't mind dancing with Barry and Zack, of course, but some of those other guys were…" Her voice faded.

"They were hitting on you. I know. Jessie told me. I couldn't sleep all night thinking about it, thinking about them. With you."

"But why? They weren't dangerous or anything. They just, you know, wanted to take me out on dates. It was kind of flattering to tell the truth. I never had so many men interested in me like that."

She looked up and saw his face had drained of color.

"You mean, you want to go out with those guys, be with them?"

"No, not really. I don't even know any of them. Is that what was worrying you?" Her forehead wrinkled. "But, why would you even think about it much less worry?"

"Because when I kept getting annoyed I started wondering why. No, that's not true. I knew why. But I'd been denying it to myself for weeks. Rationalizing it away. Couldn't you guess why during that last foxtrot, when I kept pulling you closer until we were like one body with four legs? Couldn't you see it in my eyes, how much I wanted to kiss you?"

"Really? You really wanted to kiss me? I thought I was just imagining it because…" She felt herself blushing "…because I've kind of liked you a lot for so long."

"What! Why didn't you tell me? Did Jessie know?"

"Right. Like I was going to throw myself at the guy who was spending so much of his life helping me change *my* life and scare him away. Or tell my new friend who's *also* been helping me change my life that I have the hots for her brother." Her eyes warped into shocked circles as her complexion raced from blush to scarlet. Her hands flew to cover her face. "Oh god. Did I really just say that to you?"

She didn't see his color return or the smile that softened and made his eyes shine. She just felt him move closer until their hips and thighs touched and his arms encircled her.

"Do you really feel that way about me?" he whispered, his breath warming and ticking her ear.

She nodded as she leaned into him, resting her head on his chest. Her hands dropped then snaked around him. "Mmmm. I've wanted to do that for such a long time."

One of his hands left its perch and made its way up her back to her neck. A finger caressed her collarbone, found the soft hollow in the middle, then lightly traced the curve up to her chin, where it stopped and gently urged her face to turn up to him. "And for a very long time, I've wanted to do this."

His lips touched hers and found them warm, moist, and inviting. He claimed them for his own, pressing and moving until a soft whimper of pleasure accompanied the parting of her lips, another invitation he immediately accepted. His tongue tasted her lips, then probed deeper, toying and dancing with her own. For long minutes they remained joined, each reveling in the first taste as imagination became reality, parting only when they heard footsteps on the stairs.

Her body still tingling from the kiss, Sandi desperately wanted another, but with her mother around, she was not about to put Ryan in a potentially embarrassing position. She smiled and sent a look she hoped conveyed her wish for more, later, then moved to the end of the sofa and signaled him to do the same. His answering grin let her know he understood.

"Can you keep a secret?" he asked.

Her incredulous look drew a laugh. "Right. I guess you can. But you can't tell Jessie I told you and you have to look surprised when she asks you."

"Asks me what?"

"If you've ever considered a career in children's entertainment. As a juggler. Part of a duo."

"Really?! She wants me work with her?"

"I guess it depends on whether you can learn the routines and really work as a duo. But it sounded like she was really into the idea."

Sandi's hands flew to her head and tugged her hair. "No. I'm awake. This isn't a dream. This is real. I can't believe it. I thought yesterday was the best day of my life but I was wrong. This is so much bet.." Her face drooped. "But you said you don't want to teach me anymore."

Ryan grinned. "I never said that. I said I don't want to teach you as my student anymore." His grin broadened. "I want to teach you as my girlfriend."

"Oh. *Oh!*"

All Dressed Up

Kendra didn't usually spend Friday afternoons pacing, but in a few days, she had to make a decision. Sitting behind the counter, rearranging stock, and leafing through catalogs did not provide any insight, so this afternoon she decided to try walking.

Growing up, whenever her father faced a decision, large or small, he would go for a walk. Sometimes, she would walk with him, her small legs working double-time even though he always slowed his pace when she tagged along. They would talk and laugh and later, in her teens, when she thought to ask him one day how he could think about things while they had fun, he told her the exercise and change of scenery and fun let him clear his head so his brain could work on the problem in the background.

Their walks were the thing she missed most after a heart attack took him a few weeks after her seventeenth birthday. Now twice that age, she still used walks for exercise though they never once helped her solve a problem.

Perhaps today will be the day.

She continued pacing the length of the shop, but after what felt like two miles later, she was ready to give up when the tinkle of bells interrupted her musing. She turned to find a couple coming through the door.

"Good afternoon," the woman said, "We're looking for a dress. Something old-fashioned, like, from the early nineteen hundreds."

Yes!

"Good afternoon. I'm Kendra. And I have some very nice dresses from the twenties and thirties, some even older. I'm sure several of them will fit you perfectly."

"It's not for me," the woman said, glancing at her companion, "it's for him."

Kendra watched the man blush as he rolled his eyes and shook his head.

"You're the one who wants to win first prize," the woman said to him. "This is how we'll win it." She turned back to Kendra. "It's for a costume party next weekend. Tom is determined not to lose again this year."

Kendra grinned as she looked him up and down. "Hmmm. We won't have to worry about the bust, but the waist and hips. We might need a lace-up girdle."

The woman burst out laughing as Tom's blush deepened and he blustered, "Wait a minute. I'm not wearing any girdle. It's bad enough you're getting me in a dress but if you think I'm going to…" He noticed Kendra's waving hands.

"I'm sorry," she said with a bright grin, "I really am. I was just kidding about the girdle. It's just…well, I've never had a man come in for a dress before."

"Oh. I see." He grinned. "Okay, then." He turned to the woman. "Tara, if we don't win this…"

"We will," she replied. "Trust me."

Feeling a little guilty about the joke, Kendra decided she should warn them. "Before you start looking, you should know these are real antiques, not reproductions. You can get reproductions for a couple of hundred dollars, but these are going to run five to ten times that."

"Not a problem," he said. "We've seen reproductions at other shops. We want real." The look in his eyes told Kendra he'd suffered this embarrassment several times today.

She led them to the back of the store, to a rack on which hung dozens of dresses covered with plastic to keep them pristine.

"May I call you Tom?"

"Of course. And she's Tara."

"Okay, Tom. May I assume, seriously, that you are *not* going to want to shave your legs for this party?"

"Ohmygod, what a great idea," Tara said as she looked through the rack. "You should totally shave your legs. Then you could wear this!"

She held up an early '20s red, beaded, two-piece Flapper dress. "You would look *so* hot in this I bet guys would be *hitting* on you!"

His glare drew another laugh.

"Well, he *would* look cute in that if he was our size," Kendra said, "and can fit into women's shoes…what size do you wear, Tom?"

"Eleven and a half wide."

"There's no way. We'll have to find you something that brushes the floor so you can wear your own shoes."

She moved to the end of the rack and studied several dresses before holding up one. "This is black chantilly lace over white silk. The soft, aqua velvet trim on the high collar and around bodice and the matching velvet bow were the height of fashion in the late 1890s. That's a little older than you wanted, but it's in great shape and it was custom made for a tall, stocky woman. The only difficulty might be that she was a bit on the busty side. But if your aim is to really look like a woman, big boobs wouldn't hurt. At the very least, it'll keep people from looking at your feet."

"And how, exactly, am I supposed to fill out the bust?"

Again Tara's laughter rang through the shop. "Like all women do when they need some enhancement. You stuff!"

"You mean I have to wear a bra and stuff it with tissues or something?"

"I'm afraid so, sweetie. Unless Kendra has a better solution."

"Actually, I might. Hold on." She disappeared through a curtained doorway. A minute later she returned. "This was included in a shipment of dresses from a gentleman's estate." She held up a large black brassiere into which a set of silicone breasts had been fastened. "These will give you the look and more important, the feel of real breasts. They'll move like real ones, too. And if some joker comes over and squeezes them, yell 'ouch' and slap him and he might think you really are a woman."

"See, Tom! I told you we should stop here! The woman's a genius!" She turned to Kendra. "How long have you been open? We had no idea you were here. I happened to notice your sign as we were driving by."

"I opened the shop about eight months ago."

"Well lucky for us you did. Do you think the dress and the falsies will really fit him?"

"Pretty sure, but the only way to find out is to try them on. The dressing room is over there. You'll help him with the dress?"

"Oh, dear. I don't think I'd be able to get myself into that, much less him."

Tom sighed. "Kendra, may *I* assume you've seen the occasional man in a tee shirt and boxers?"

A bashful grin preceded, "Yes, the occasional one."

"Then let's just do this. And Tara, pay close attention so we won't need phone support from her next Saturday."

The fitting went well, and even Tom laughed when he saw himself in the dress, complete with a 38D bust. "Now we just need to get Tara a tuxedo. Any chance you have one from the same period?"

"As a matter of fact, I have one I wore to a Halloween party last year. I found it in a Salvation Army store, of all places. It's what got me interested in vintage and antique clothes. Black tail coat, black trousers and suspenders, white dress shirt with a wing-tip collar, white vest with lapels and a scooped front, and a white bow tie. Very 1890s. I even have the top hat and period shoes, though they've been resoled. They're a seven and a half."

"I wear a seven, but a little tissue in the toe will take care of that. May I see it?"

"Yes, but it's in storage. I'll bring it in tomorrow and if you like how you look in it, you can borrow it for the party. But *only* if you promise to take pictures for me of the two of you all dressed up."

"Are you serious?"

She nodded. "I can't sell it. It was my inspiration for the business. But if you folks are buying the dress and boobs, I'll be happy to let you borrow it. It really is the perfect outfit to go with this dress. The only thing I don't have is white gloves from the period. They got ruined at the party. You'll both need those but you can get reproductions at Glowner's on Dustin Ave. Tom, make sure you get gloves that will cover the ends of the sleeves. Ladies showed very little skin back then. And you'll be getting a period wig?"

"That's our next stop."

"Good. Do you have a hat?"

"I need a hat?"

"A lady would never travel or arrive at a party without a hat. I have three that might work with that dress."

"You have to be kidding," Tom said, as Kendra removed the three hats from their boxes. Tara stepped back a pace and covered her mouth with her hand, holding in another laugh.

"These were very fashionable during that period. I can show you pictures or you can google them if you want. Actually, these three are pretty reserved."

"There is no way I'm wearing that…that flower arrangement or that thing with the bird on it so I guess I'm stuck with the velvet thing with the feathers."

Twenty minutes later, sale made, Kendra watched two happy customers walk out the door with their purchase. She looked at the credit slip, then up and said, "Did you send them, Dad? Are you still looking out for me after all these years?" Her eyes returned to the slip. "However it happened, I guess I'm open for at least another couple of months."

~ ~ ~

The next day, Tara arrived late in the morning. When she stepped out of the dressing room, she glowed with pleasure.

"This is wonderful, Kendra. We are *so* going to win the couples' prize. I don't know how to thank you."

"You could tell your friends about the shop."

"Ha! I already did that. I took a bunch of your business cards yesterday and already gave out some. But if anyone shows up wanting to know what you sold us, you have to promise not to tell."

Kendra crossed her heart and followed with a Girl Scout salute.

"And would it be okay if I left this all here until next Friday. I'm afraid if I take it home now, something might happen to it and I'd never forgive myself."

~ ~ ~

The following week proved to be Kendra's best-to-date. Four couples, three women, and one guy came in, thanks to Tara, and all walked out satisfied customers. Only one woman asked about Tara's and Tom's outfits but she accepted Kendra's, "I'm sorry, but it's a store policy to never discuss other customers."

By Friday morning, she was anxious to see Tara again so she could thank her for all the referrals but noon rolled around without her. A couple came in just before two-thirty. When they left an hour later, he carried a peach-colored leisure suit with wide bell-bottoms and a red, white and purple paisley polyester shirt. She decided on an electric-blue mini-dress with long flared sleeves, white fishnet stockings, a pair of clear, Lucite sandals with six-inch heels, and a wig that almost exactly matched the color of the dress. They hadn't mentioned Tara or Tom but she assumed they would be attending the same party since Halloween was still months away.

She wondered if Tara forgot and debated whether or not she should call her when the clock struck five, but decided she would call in the morning if she didn't show up by eleven.

At six, she locked the front door and flipped over the sign to "Closed." Then she walked to the back of the store, through the curtained doorway to the left side of the storage room, and opened the door to what was once a large office or break room with a little kitchenette, but was now her studio apartment. She looked around and sighed.

One of these days I really need to clean this place.

Moving from her cozy one-bedroom apartment to a converted office had been the most difficult part of opening the business. But it made no sense to pay two rents when living here would reduce her monthly obligations by almost fourteen-hundred dollars. And all it had taken was eight hundred dollars to install the shower.

She fished her phone out of her pocket and dialed her best friend.

"Well, what do you know!" Bethany said. "Is this really Kendra or has my phone malfunctioned?"

"Hi, Beth. It's only been two days, so get over yourself. Do you have a date tonight?"

"No. Nobody loves me but you. Want to come over and drink too much wine and watch some silly movie and complain about men?"

"Love to. I'll even bring the wine. I had a really good week and I feel like celebrating."

And celebrate they did, killing three and a half bottles of Zinfandel while crying their way through *The Notebook* and determining with absolute certainty that there were no more good men available anywhere in the city or surrounding suburbs.

~ ~ ~

When Kendra opened her eyes the next morning, the glare sent ice picks of pain shooting through her head.

Oh, crap. I passed out at Beth's.

She covered her eyes with her hand and ever-so-slowly allowed light to reach them until she could see without it hurting.

And I forgot to take some aspirin and drink two glasses of water.

Her throbbing temples told her that.

She lifted her head enough to see Beth asleep at the other end of the sofa. Despite the pain, she smiled as she remembered last night's dueling diatribes and wondered if certain men in the area felt their ears burning, or other parts throbbing from verbal kicks. She pulled out her phone to check the time.

Oh crap!

It was ten past eight. She had fifty minutes to get back to the store, shower and change, and open the door at nine.

She would have only been five minutes late if she had been willing to run out barefoot, but since no customer ever showed up before ten, she spent the extra three minutes donning socks and sneakers. Of course, customers were waiting. Three of them, a man and two women. Neither was Tara.

The man chose his 1940's G-man outfit in less than fifteen minutes. Then he stood or walked around until quarter to eleven doing business on his phone while the women tried on dozens of outfits. Both settled on replica flapper dresses, one red, the other green. With scarves and headgear and jewelry, the total sale was nearly twelve hundred dollars.

"Not a bad way to start the day!" Kendra said aloud once the door closed behind the trio.

The busy start coupled with painkillers, water, and coffee had faded about half of her hangover. She checked in with Beth, who said she slept until after ten, then crawled from the couch to the kitchen to make a huge Bloody Mary, and was now sipping it while soaking in a hot bath. They relived a few choice moments from the previous evening until the store phone rang and Kendra said goodbye.

"Yesterday Once More, this is Kendra. May I help you?"

"Excellent, you're open. Kendra, this is Tom Claymore. I'm in a real jam here and I'm hoping you can help me out."

"I'll try. What's the problem?"

"The problem is that Tara is sick. She's been sick for three days and there's no way she's able to go to the party tonight. She suggested I call you to see if you'd be willing to accompany me tonight. There'll be good food, good music, dancing. The affair is at the Oakwood Country Club. It's the annual costume fundraiser for the club's charities. And since I'm on the board, I can't blow it off. And I don't want to anyway because we finally have the killer costumes that will win the couples' contest. So, would you be willing to don the tux Tara was going to wear, plus a wig and matching beard, and be my escort to the party tonight?"

"I…I've never been to a country club affair before. I don't know what to say."

"Say yes. Please. Because either way, I'm going to need your help getting into this dress. I don't think the cleaning lady will be on-board with seeing me in my underwear."

"I…look, can I call you back in fifteen minutes? I have a headache and I have to do something here. Fifteen minutes tops."

"Are you okay? You're not getting sick, too?"

"No, I'm fine. Fifteen minutes. Bye."

As soon as she ended the call, she whipped out her cellphone. "Beth! You are not going to believe what just happened."

After hearing the details, Beth said, "So what's the problem? Go! How often do you get invited to a country club?"

"But he's married. And I like his wife."

"God, Kendra, he's not asking you to sleep with him. You're just going to eat and maybe dance a little and have a good time along with a lot of rich folks."

"But…"

"Ken, if you don't want to go, tell him you know someone who will. Me."

"You wouldn't fit in the tux."

"Then tell him you'll go. If you pass this up I'll never forgive you."

When Tom heard she would accompany him, his relief and happiness reached through the phone and made her smile. "The cocktail reception begins at seven, but as a board member, I have to be there by six. What time do you close the shop?"

"Six, but I can close earlier, at four."

"That'd be great. I live in Grafston, the club is in Rockford, and your shop is in the middle. Where do you live?"

"I…you can just pick me up at the shop. The outfit's here anyway."

"Hmmm…I was going to send a car to get you and bring you here to help me dress, but maybe it would be better to meet you at the store and get dressed there. I'll have the makeup guy come at three and I'll be at your place by the time you close."

"Okay. And please tell Tara I hope she's feeling better soon."

The afternoon seemed to drag despite two more couples coming in. Only one ended up buying, but the woman opted for the red flapper dress Tara had teased Tom with and the man bought a replica Civil War uniform even though it was a size too big for him.

As the clock neared four, Kendra was pacing the store from front to back as her nervousness increased.

What was I thinking agreeing to this? I'm not one of this crowd. Who will I talk to? What will I talk about? What do I know about golf and spas and European vacations? But it will be an adventure. And I haven't been on a date for, oh god, almost six months! I am so pathetic. And this isn't a date. I'm just helping a customer and then he'll go home to his wife and I'll come back here and wish I weren't such a...

"Stop! You're making yourself crazy!"

"Well I wish you wouldn't. I liked the funny, sassy you I met last week."

Oh no! Tom! How did I not hear the bells?

When she turned, her hand flew to cover her open mouth but couldn't cover her surprise. "Oh, my! I can't believe it. You look beautiful. You are *so* going to look like a real woman once you're dressed."

Tom heaved a sigh of relief. "I was afraid you were going to laugh when you saw me."

"No way! That makeup guy is a genius!"

"I'm happy to hear that. So where should we do this? Dressing room?"

"Actually, I want to take a shower first."

"You have a shower in the shop?"

Crap. Now he finds out what a loser I am.

She explained about the converted office and was surprised when he nodded thoughtfully and said, "That makes good sense. The first year of any business is the toughest and anything that saves cash for the business increases the chance for success." The admiration she saw in his eyes made her spirits soar.

She led him through the back to the studio, apologized for the mess, told him to make himself at home, and headed for the bathroom. Ten minutes later, as she was toweling her hair, it occurred to her that the tux was still hanging on a hook in the apartment and she had not even thought to bring in underwear. "Oh well," she said to her reflection, "I've seen him in his underwear, I guess he can see me in a towel."

Kendra opened the door to find Tom on the sofa. He glanced up from the magazine and froze at the sight of her in such a state of dishabille.

"Sorry. I forgot a few things." She padded barefoot to the dresser where she fished out the pair of gray, men's boxer briefs she bought to wear under the tux last year, a pair of black socks, and the two, small sports bras she would use to compress her breasts. Then she retrieved the tux, all the while aware of his eyes following her every move.

As she neared the bathroom, she heard him say, "Uhh…you wouldn't consider going to the party in that costume, would you? Wet hair and all. I mean, wow! You look amazing like that. Beautiful."

Her heart skipped a beat even as she felt the color rising in her cheeks. She turned to find a genuine look of wonder on his face and rewarded it with a smile. "I will if you will. But it would be a shame to waste that outfit you bought. And I'm not sure half-naked bath mates will win any prizes."

He sighed, clearly disappointed, which did more for her ego than all the self-help books she ever read.

Calm down, Kendra. He's just being a guy. A married guy.

She began to turn away.

"Wait! I'm sorry about that remark. Totally inappropriate. And you shouldn't have to dress in the bathroom. I'll go wait out front."

When she stepped through the curtains awhile later, she saw he unpacked everything and laid it on the counter.

"Wow! You look great in that." He held up a hand, partially blocking his view. "From the neck down you really look like a guy. What happened to your..ummm…."

"Breasts?" She explained after he nodded.

He handed her a small box containing the wig, beard and moustache, the glue to apply it, and an instruction sheet. "I hope it all fits. It should. You and Tara are about the same size."

She removed the items from the box and said, "This is professional stuff."

"Of course. You can't win first prize with hair from a joke shop."

"I guess you're right."

It took her nearly twenty minutes to apply the facial hair and wig, but it was time well spent.

Tom's eyes took her in and he grinned. "If I didn't know you were a woman under there…amazing. My turn, I guess."

She followed him into the dressing room, then turned her back as he began unbuttoning his shirt. She heard him chuckle.

"Kendra, you've already seen me undressed. There won't be anything new this time."

She turned back with a sheepish grin. "Actually, there will be. You really should wear the falsies without an undershirt. That way, they sort of stick to your chest and won't slide around as they did last week."

He nodded as he stepped out of his trousers. Kendra forced herself to keep her eyes on his face. Then he pulled off his undershirt revealing a hairy, muscular chest.

Oh my! Tara is a lucky woman.

"How the hell do you women do this?" he complained. He had slipped the bra with the falsies over his arms, settled it against his chest, and was straining as he tried to figure out how to fasten the back strap.

She laughed. "It's easy. You just put the hooks through the eyes. Here, let me."

A few minutes later, he was in the dress. Kendra picked up the beautifully curled wig and had him sit while she adjusted it over his short hair, using a dozen bobby pins to make sure it remained in place. Finally, she removed the hat from its box and bobby-pinned it in place. Then, they slipped on the gloves.

"Ohmygod," she gushed as they stood side-by-side in front of the mirror wall. "We look fantastic!"

"I have to admit we do. Thank you, Kendra."

"It's nothing, really I just…wait!"

She turned and hurried from the dressing room. When she returned, she held a light-blue parasol and a matching fan. "These aren't exactly the same color as the trim on the dress, but they're close enough that a woman back then would use them."

"What am I supposed to do with them?"

"You hold the parasol in your left hand. It rests on your shoulder. The fan you use to fan yourself. Or hide your face as you giggle, should some attractive and eligible young man look your way. Here, let me show you."

She opened the parasol and fan and demonstrated their proper use. Then he tried them and grudgingly admitted they did enhance the costume.

As they rode to the country club, Tom filled in more details of the evening. After the board meeting, which would only take ten or fifteen minutes, they and the other board members and their spouses would gather in the ballroom for a toast to a successful evening.

"Then we all take up stations just inside the doors to greet the guests as they arrive. But don't worry. All you'll have to do is stand there looking manly."

She laughed and asked, "Will you be talking in falsetto?"

"No," he said, his voice suddenly changing pitch and becoming soft and feminine, "I don't think that will be necessary. I think this voice will do just fine, don't you?"

Kendra was so astonished she clapped. "That's wonderful! How do you do that?"

"Practice, darling," he said, still in character, "lots and lots of practice." He switched back to his normal voice. "I was in the drama club in an all-boys prep school.

And I minored in theater in college just to annoy my parents."

They talked about school and then business until the limo turned into a long driveway. Tom reminded the driver they would be going in at the right rear.

"Rick, is that Charlie at the door?"

"I think so, sir."

Tom shifted into 'the voice.' "Let's have a little fun."

As the limo coasted to a stop, Kendra said, "Wait. Switch seats so I can get out first. And give me the parasol. And use the fan."

When the driver opened the door, she slid out, opened the parasol, and held it up with one hand while extending the other to assist her companion from the limo. Then she handed 'her' the parasol and whispered, "Do your thing."

With Kendra at his side, Tom strode regally up the walk. As they approached the door, Charlie said, "I'm sorry folks. You'll have to use the front entrance. Only board members can go in this way tonight."

Adding a dose of honey to the voice, Tom said, "Oh dear, I really *must* take care of some female issues soon. Won't you please make an exception just this once?"

Charlie truly looked pained when he replied, "I really am sorry, but I'll lose my job if I let anyone in but board members."

Tom nudged Kendra with his foot, a signal she took to mean *jump in anytime*. Deepening her voice as much as she dared, she said, "See here, my good man, Lady Agatha Dendermonde deCrevecoeur is not accustomed to being refused. How can you deny a lady in need? What sort of gentleman would do such a thing?"

They could tell Charlie wished he was anywhere else but there at the moment, so when he pulled out his radio, Tom took pity, moved the fan away from his face, and said, "Charlie. Look closely."

He did. He stared for nearly thirty seconds before the features under the makeup came into focus. "Mr. Claymore? Is that you? I must be dreaming."

"It's no dream. And I'm sorry we did that. I wanted to test the costume and makeup and it appears it passed with flying colors. Thank you, Charlie. Please don't tell anyone else who's in this dress. I plan to have a bit more fun before the night's over."

Charlie held the door for them and Kendra got her first look at how the other half lived. The rich wood doors, floors, and trim, the crystal light fixtures, the tables with vases of fresh flowers, even the plush carpet runner oozed money.

"Is this a service entrance or something?"

"It's the staff entrance, though any member who parks on this side can use it. We're using it today because it's the quickest way to the ballroom and conference room."

If this is the staff entrance, what does the main entrance look like? I guess I'll find out later.

They stopped at the conference room and found it empty so they continued on to the ballroom. Kendra reached for the door handle and said, "Ladies first" with as deep a voice as she could manage.

"Thank you, my good man. Let me do the talking inside."

The sound of the door opening turned a dozen heads at the other end of the room and the sight of a tall, busty woman being escorted by a smaller, bearded man set heads pivoting back and forth as they wondered, in whispers, who the newcomers might be.

About twenty feet from the group, Kendra nodded their way as Tom said, in character, "Oh dear, Ken. I fear we have arrived much too early. There's hardly anyone here. How tiresome."

One of the group detached himself and met them halfway. "Good evening, folks. I'm Dan Crescente. I'm one of the board members here at the club. I'm afraid you've wandered into the ballroom before it's ready to open."

"Wander? My good man, Lady Agatha Dendermonde deCrevecoeur does not wander." As he spoke, Tom noted which two board members had not arrived. "I was asked to grace your little soirée with my presence by our good friend Doctor James Worthington." He turned and said, "How am I doing with my American, Kenny dear?"

Kendra's heart skipped a beat. Outside with a guard was one thing, but she wasn't prepared for a speaking part in front of a crowd.

Oh, well. Keep it short.

"Quite well, Lady Agatha. Almost like a native."

Tom redoubled his fanning as he walked by Dan and approached the group, who stood mesmerized by the odd duo. "Splendid. I almost *feel* like a native."

He surveyed the ladies and their costumes, lingering on the red flapper dress Tara teased him with last week. "My, my. You look positively smashing in that, my dear. What is your name?"

"Ahh…Deborah Turindo…uh…Lady Agatha."

"I am pleased to make your acquaintance." She let out a deep sigh. "Oh, is there *anything* I wouldn't give to have a figure that could fit in that dress. What do you think, Kenny? Would it be worth the summer house in Derbyshire?"

"With or without the sixty-four hundred acres, Milady?"

"With, of course."

"I believe Lord deCrevecoeur would consider it a bargain, Milady."

Before Tom could choose his next target, the door across the hall opened. "Oh, good," he heard Dan mutter. "James and Phil are here." He walked off to meet them.

Tom knew the jig was up, but turned to face the final two board members. He did not want to miss James's reaction when Dan told him who was waiting for him.

The doctor's "What?" echoed through the ballroom.

His pace quickened, annoyance creasing his face, but Tom did not give him an opening. He hurried forward as quickly as was ladylike and said, "James! How wonderful to see you after so many years." He saw a flicker of doubt and went in for the kill. "I was so happy when I heard your secretary had called mine to invite me. How do you like my American? I've been practicing just for you!"

With that, Tom took the final two steps and with the parasol in one hand and the fan in the other, threw his arms around his bewildered friend and hugged him. Then he backed off a step, took him by the shoulders and, with his face inches away, said, "My goodness, you haven't changed a bit. How do I look after all this time?" Then he waited.

To his credit, it took the doctor less than ten seconds before he grinned and said, "You son-of-a-bitch, Claymore. You son-of-a-bitch."

Behind him, Tom could hear laughter and exclamations of disbelief.

"You really had me going. Where did you find that getup? Damn! And that voice!" He looked past Tom. "Tara, is that you under there? Did you arrange this?" He shook his head. "Remarkable. If I didn't know your face, Tom, I'd never have guessed you were not a woman."

Tom waved everyone over, explained about Tara's illness, and introduced Kendra to the board and their wives. Then Tom and the others headed off for their meeting, leaving Kendra with the ladies.

She found herself the center of attention as Deborah and two others who bought their outfits at her shop sang its praises to the others. But after ten minutes of non-stop questions and thank yous, it was time for a change of subject.

"I was just wondering," she began as she swept her gaze across the group, "why there are no women on the board?"

Eight mouths began talking at once until Worthington's wife, Johana, shushed them all. "That is a bit of a sore point in the club at the moment, Kendra. It was only four years ago that women were permitted full membership on their own. And we've all been lobbying our husbands, who *all* claim to have no problem with women serving on the board, but somehow, when nominations are announced each year, women don't seem to get enough votes to make the cut. But we're not giving up. Some of us are determined to get a woman on the board, however long it takes."

The men chose that moment to return from their meeting. They were followed by two waiters with trays of champagne. It fell to James Worthington, the chairman, to give the toast.

"Ladies and gentleman, one hundred twelve years ago, this club was founded by August Archibald and nineteen other prominent citizens for two purposes, to provide a place to relax after a hard day's work, and to provide a place where those of their neighbors who were in need could go for assistance. As the club grew, so did its mission, and last year we were able to raise nine point four million dollars for the various charitable endeavors we sponsor in and around the city. This year, I, for one, would like to see us top ten million. So, if you will all raise your glasses…to success!"

A chorus repeated, "To success!"

A waiter appeared carrying a large, glass bowl into which Worthington placed a check for fifty-thousand dollars. The waiter stopped in front of each gentleman who likewise deposited checks of varying amounts. When the last had settled on the bottom, James said, "Thank you all for your contributions of money and time. Now let's get this party started!"

The door through which everyone had entered opened again and the musicians, who set up and tuned their instruments earlier, filed in and took their places as two couples stationed themselves at each of the four sets of double doors. The Worthingtons watched it all from the center of the dance floor. When everyone was ready, James nodded to the conductor, then to the waitstaff who pushed open the doors to the strains of the opening fanfare from *Also sprach Zarathustra*.

Kendra had little to do for most of the next hour other than stand next to Tom, smile through her beard, and do her best to refrain from laughing at the expressions of guests as they tried to figure out who was greeting them, often by name. It was a relief when the orchestra stopped playing long enough for the conductor to request that guests take their seats for supper. Tom led her to their table and laughed when she, being a perfect gentleman, held the chair for Lady Agatha.

The thought of having to make conversation with incredibly wealthy and, in many cases, very talented strangers set her nerves on edge from the moment the doors opened, so she was grateful to discover the other four couples at the table were as easy to talk to as was Tom. Apparently, jokes, amusing stories, and laughter were the order of the evening. Kendra was quickly drawn in and having a wonderful time. Once, as her head pivoted to follow a conversation, she got the impression Tom was watching her instead of whoever was speaking, but when she leaned close and asked if anything was wrong, he assured her he was just happy to see her enjoying herself.

The meal was amazing, making the fare at several upscale weddings Kendra attended seem, in comparison, like diner food. But by the time dessert was being served, Kendra could not even look at it.

During the meal, the orchestra played selections from the Big Band era and had just transitioned from *Little Brown Jug* to *Fly Me To The Moon* when Kendra touched heads with Tom and whispered, "Can you dance ballroom?"

At his nod, she stood, held out her hand and asked Lady Agatha, "Would you be so kind as to honor me with a dance or two?"

As she led him to the floor, she told him, "I hope you can follow."

"What?"

"Have you forgotten? You're the lady. I'm the gentleman. Men ask and men lead."

A grin lit his face. "Right you are, sir."

When they reached the center of the dance floor, she swung him out, then reeled him in and led him into a foxtrot. They quickly became the center of attention as they glided across the floor and when the song came to a close, many of the guests applauded.

"I wonder if the applause is for the dancing or that I didn't trip and fall in this dress?"

Kendra laughed, and even through the beard, Tom was struck by how it lit up her face. Then she almost shouted, "Yes! It's swing time" as the opening notes of *In the Mood* reached her. "If you can keep from tripping on those skirts this time, even I'll applaud you!"

She soon realized Tom was at least as good a dancer as she was, probably better given he was performing in a dress designed for little more than a gentle waltz. They mixed single steps, triple steps, spins, turns, and everything else they could think of into a dance so energetic and varied that when it was over, the orchestra had to wait for the applause to die down before they could begin the next song.

Kendra bowed and Tom curtsied their thanks for the ovation, while gently teasing each other, and when the orchestra resumed with *Again*, she could almost hear her mother singing the song she played countless times on the family stereo. She led Tom in slow turns as other couples joined them on the floor.

A once in a lifetime thrill that will never happen again. How fitting.

Then she wished she could plaster herself against him this one time, but anything like that would surely get back to Tara.

Calm down, girl. Don't let all the glitter go to your head.

As the evening wore on, the dance floor stayed crowded. The orchestra advanced through the decades, playing rock and roll, disco, jazz, country, R&B, even orchestral arrangements of some heavy metal, punk, and hip hop. Kendra danced to it all with a partner who matched her step for step, move for move. Each time the music slowed and they moved close, the urge to move closer returned. She resisted, but gave in to quiet fantasies of what he might be like when his guard was down. She felt herself blushing in shame after realizing how jealous she was of Tara and her good fortune in meeting and marrying such a wonderful man.

Oh, well. Every girl deserves a Cinderella night, even if she does have to wear a beard to get it.

Much too soon for her liking, midnight approached

and the musicians set down their instruments for the costume contest.

"Ladies and gentleman," the Chairman began, "on behalf of the Oakwood family of charities, I want to thank you all for attending this evening.

"Our costume contest is about to begin. We will be awarding ten prizes again this year and, as is traditional, our wait staff has randomly selected seven of their members to serve as judges.

"Please remain seated until I call your table. Then, proceed as couples to the table to my left where you'll be given numbers. From there, go to the flag at the edge of the dance floor and walk slowly toward the judges on the opposite side, show them your numbers, then return to your seats. If anyone does not care to participate, simply remain seated when your table is called.

"Are there any questions? No? Then let's begin with table number one. And while you are waiting, if you have not already done so, please take this opportunity to pull out your checkbook or take one of the pledge slips you'll find on your table and fill it out with as generous a donation as you can manage. Seal it in one of the envelopes on your table and hold it up and one of the wait staff will deposit it in the fishbowl to my right.

"Once again, thank you all for your generosity and good luck to everyone!"

The contest proceeded quickly as comments, hoots, and whistles were directed at various participants. When it was their turn to walk the floor, Tom did so with parasol open and his other hand resting on Kendra's arm.

It pleased her to see the outfits she sold participants get enthusiastic receptions. Deborah Turindo, in the red flapper dress, received enough hoots and whistles that Kendra could tell her husband wasn't especially pleased. She was too nervous when she met her earlier to give any thought to how she looked in it, but now she realized Deborah had the perfect body for it and had accessorized with shoes, stockings with garters, jewelry, and a headband that would have turned heads when the dress was new, as was happening now. Even though her husband wore a Brooks Brothers tux instead of a matching period suit, she thought they had a chance to take first prize.

She glanced at Tom and sighed as he spoke with the couple next to him.

I should call Tara tomorrow and thank her for letting me go in her place. Who knows, maybe I'll make a friend. But then I'd be seeing him all the time.

She repeated the sigh.

All conversation stopped when the chairman stepped up to the microphone to announce the winners. Numbers ten through four all received Honorable Mention plaques along with generous gift cards from a few upscale restaurants in the city.

"Our top three winners will receive the small, medium, and large trophies you see on the table, as well as an assortment of gift cards to area restaurants and shops. In addition, third place will win a new set of golf clubs from the pro shop plus a monthly meal for four in the Club dining room. Second place wins the golf clubs plus a weekly meal for four, and first place takes home the clubs, the weekly meals, and a waiver of one year's membership dues.

"So, without further ado…" He tore the seal on the folded paper. "…our third place winners are…George and Rosemary Manuel!"

The couple, dressed as the Jolly Green Giant and Little Sprout, were all smiles as they made their way to the stage.

The chairman opened the next paper. "Finishing

second, Chaz and Tulia Montgomery!" A Roman Gladiator and Slave Girl stood, took a bow, and proceeded to the stage to applause.

Kendra had been sitting with her fingers crossed as the winners were being announced. As each was disclosed, she felt competing twinges of disappointment it was not her and Tom and elation they were still in the running for first place. But in a few seconds, she would feel a surge of one or the other. It was down to all or nothing.

"And now..." He pretended to struggle with the seal on the paper, drawing some laughs from the guests."...wow, big surprise...or not...ladies and gentleman, please stand..." Most of the room did. "...and make some noise for this year's first place winners...Tom Claymore and Kendra McFarland!"

"Yes!" she cried as she jumped up and down with delight. And when Tom turned to congratulate her, she jumped forward and threw her arms around him in a joyous hug. His arms encircled her and pressed her close for a few seconds before releasing her. She wished it could have been longer, but took that as a cue and let go. Then they shared a grin and strolled to the stage, arm in arm, to rousing applause.

Kendra replayed the entire night in her head as she sat next to Tom on the ride home. She expected the costume awards would be the finale, but instead, the party picked up where it left off, with more dancing, more champagne, and more fun. Now, it was after three. She was tired, but could not remember ever feeling happier. Their matching trophies sat on the seat between them and though she knew it was wrong, she wished she and Tom were sitting as close as the trophies.

Oh, well. At least the Prince is escorting Cinderella

home in this fairy tale. But then he goes home to his wife.

She sighed.

"Are you okay?"

"Yes. Just tired. It's been years since I danced that much. Speaking of which, you really surprised me. Most men are lucky to be able to shuffle around on a dance floor but you knew all the moves, and then some! More theater training?"

He closed his eyes and nodded. "Yes, though I didn't come to it naturally. Voices were easy, but dancing, that was a challenge. It took a long time for me to lose my second left foot."

Kendra laughed. "Well, you'd never know it watching you now."

"Thank you. But speaking of surprises, you've been full of them tonight."

"Really? How so?"

"Well, it began with what you told me about the apartment in the store. There are not a lot of people who would have recognized that potential or been willing to sacrifice as you've done to give their business a better chance to grow. That's pretty impressive."

Pleasure at the compliment from someone so accomplished in business warmed her from head to toe.

"Then there was your performance when we first arrived at the club." He laughed. "Lady Agatha. That was inspired! Which reminds me, I'll have to apologize again to Charlie for what we did. But continuing on, you next surprised me with your poise and grace as we were greeting guests and then at how relaxed you were during dinner because you seemed a little nervous when we started out. Then, there was your dancing ability.

"It seemed like you kept surprising me all night and, well, I just wanted to thank you yet again and say how happy I am that it was you who filled in for Tara tonight. I expect she'll be quite jealous when I tell her about the party.

"And here we are. Perfect timing. I'll get the door, Rick."

The limo rolled to a stop.

"I know it's late, but would you mind if I used the dressing room to change out of this getup, which I'm desperately hoping you'll help me out of?"

Tom followed her into the shop and then to the dressing room where she undid fasteners for the dress and falsies.

"Now, just pull your arms out of the sleeves, slide the front off your shoulders and let the dress fall to the floor. Then you can just step out of it. I'll wait out front for you."

When he appeared several minutes later, the dress hanging over one arm, he held out the falsies with his other hand. "Do you have a bag I can put these in? And a hanger for the dress?"

She produced both along with a garment bag. "You know you can't take this to a regular dry cleaners?" She laughed at his blank stare. "There's a place over on Lynch Ave. that specializes in cleaning and restoration. I don't think you did any damage, but if they find anything loose or torn, they'll fix it. I can have them pick it up here Monday if you like."

"That will be great, Kendra. Thanks. But can I ask one last favor?" He reached in his pocket for a jar. "May I use your bathroom for a few minutes to get all this makeup off my face?"

"Of course. Come in the apartment and use that one."

Again she led the way and flipped on the lights. "You'll see the box of tissues, but there's a roll of soft paper towels under the sink. I think you'll have better luck getting the heavy stuff off with those."

She settled into a chair, expecting to have ten or fifteen minutes to reminisce, but he surprised her by reappearing in just over five. "That was fast!"

He held up the jar. "The makeup guy gave me this. It's some professional stuff you can use for everything. Costs a fortune, but is so worth it. When I used to do theater, it would take me almost as long to get all the makeup off as it took me to put it on." He glanced at his watch. "Ouch. I think it's time to get home."

This time, he led her to the front where he grabbed the bag with the falsies. She unlocked the front door and held it open, but he remained still for a few seconds. Then he said, "Kendra, I feel like I owe you an apology. When Tara and I came in that first day, I thought of you as a simple store clerk. Not that there is anything wrong with being a store clerk, but I let a stereotype filter my opinion.

"I'm ashamed to say that the reason you kept surprising me all night was because my expectations were…well…I was not expecting someone so accomplished and personable. You taught me something about myself tonight." He sighed. "I guess the bottom line is I'm sorry for misjudging you and I want to thank you for opening my eyes. Besides being beautiful, you're an amazing woman and it was a privilege to spend the evening with you."

And before she realized what was happening, he leaned in and gave her a quick, gentle kiss on the lips.

"Huh," he said, grinning. "That was the first time I ever kissed someone with a beard." He rubbed his face and laughed. "Kind of scratchy." Then he vanished into the limo and was gone.

~ ~ ~

Kendra's eyes snapped open at the sound of the phone ringing.

Tom!

She shook her head, feeling foolish.

Why would he be calling me?

"Hello," she mumbled into the receiver.

"Uh-oh. Did I wake you?"

"Yes, Beth, you did. What time is it?"

"A little after eight."

She groaned. "Call me back at eleven. I didn't get to sleep until after four."

"Oh-ho!"

"No, nothing like that. Call me later and we'll have lunch and I'll tell you all about it.

"He kissed you! I don't believe it!"

Kendra nodded. "I know. It's funny. All night I kept thinking about him, feeling jealous of Tara, wanting to be close to him, even kiss him. I knew it would never happen, but it was this beautiful fantasy night and I looked forward to reliving it in my head for a long time. And then he said all those really nice things and my ego was soaring. Then he kissed me, and for a few seconds, my heart really did flutter, but as soon as he turned away I realized the kiss ruined it. I don't know. Maybe he meant it as friendly, but friendly is a kiss on the cheek. A married man has no business kissing anyone but his wife on the lips."

She sighed. "I should have known. My coach didn't turn into a pumpkin at midnight. My prince turned into a frog at four A.M."

~ ~ ~

Apparently, word of her part in the win at the fundraiser got around, for Monday morning brought with it to the store a steady stream of people. Some bought, some just looked, some congratulated her, some didn't, but just seeing so many people in the shop in so short a time was enough to make Kendra's day.

Just after one, a woman came in asking if the picture in the newspaper was really her. Suddenly, the rush of people made sense. There, on page two, was a photo of her and Tom holding their trophies.

"Can you make me look like that," the woman asked, "but with a more modern suit and no beard?"

Kendra struggled to keep from rolling her eyes and laughing. "I think we might be able to find something you'll like. Are you going to a costume party?"

"No." The woman blushed. "My boyfriend and I like to, you know, role-play a little."

Okay! Not pursuing that!

"What about a gangster? Like in one of the old movies. Or even something more recent, like *The Godfather?*"

"That would be perfect! My name is Donna. I could be Donna Corleone!"

By five-thirty, Kendra was happy to see the store empty. She had been on the go all day and welcomed the opportunity to perch on her stool and relax. She opened her laptop and began searching eBay and other sites for vintage clothing. Three bids later, she heard the door bells tinkle and looked up find Tom coming in.

Oh, god.

Despite his ruining her fantasy, her stomach did flips at the sight of his smile.

"Hello, again! I wasn't sure I'd make it before you closed. How are you today?"

Small talk? He wants to make small talk?

"I'm tired, but fine. The store was busy today, thanks to our picture in the paper."

"I saw that. Tara says hello, by the way, and thank you for taking her place."

Darn. I was going to call her yesterday, wasn't I?

"I hope she's feeling better."

"She is and should be feeling up to going out in another day or two. The docs finally decided it was some kind of virus."

Might as well get this over with, whatever it is.

"So what brings you here this afternoon?"

She watched his face change from happy to thoughtful.

"Well, ummm…the thing is, I haven't been able to stop thinking about you. All that stuff I said in the limo and in the shop after the party, I really meant every word of it. You're different from the other women I know. More real, I guess. And maybe that's what surprised me most, because at the party, I kept catching myself watching you at dinner. And when we were dancing slow, I had to fight the urge to pull you close to me. That kind of thing never happened to me before. Well, that's not exactly true. It has happened, but the other times were different. They were just physical. But with you it was more. Physical, too, but more. I don't know. I'm making a mess of this."

He shook his head.

"What I'm trying to say is that I'd like to see you again. Socially. Dinner. Movie. Play. Opera. Walk in the park. Whatever you like. I just want the chance to get to know you. To let you get to know me. See if something clicks."

Geez. Is this guy for real? Could this be the first time he's thought about cheating on Tara? Let's see.

"Tom, I had a really nice time with you Saturday, but why would you want to date someone like me?"

His face clouded. "I don't understand the question. I'm a man, you're a woman I like a lot. Seems pretty basic to me."

"Well, sure. Dating, sex, it's all very basic. But why with me? Surely someone in your position knows lots of gorgeous, willing women. Why pass them up for me?"

"I told you. Look, I've dated…been with a fair number of women, but someone in my position, as you put it, successful and wealthy, attracts women who, despite anything else they may see in me, see the dollar signs behind me. Then there are the women who have money of their own. With them, getting together is a business deal. You're different. From what I've seen the two times we've been together, you have all the good qualities of all those other women and something more, something real, the determination to take risks, to start something and build it, and the willingness to sacrifice and do whatever it takes to make your vision a reality and a success. All that is very rare, at least in my experience. And so I'd like to spend time with you, get to know you."

"And Tara wouldn't care if you and I were…dating?"

"I don't know why she should. She likes you."

Oh! Swingers! Now it all makes sense. But I'm tired and hungry. Time to end this.

"Look, Tom. I'm very flattered that you think so much of me, and I will admit I find you interesting and attractive, but there's just one thing that seems like an insurmountable problem to me."

"What's that?"

She smiled as sweetly as she could manage. "I don't go out with married men."

There!

She was not sure which of many possible reactions she would see on his face, but shock and confusion were not even on the list.

"What? Married! Who am I supposed to be married to?"

"To Tara, of course."

He began laughing so hard he had to steady himself with a hand on the counter. After half-a-minute, he managed to choke out, "I'm not married to Tara" before laughter consumed him again for a few seconds. "Why in the world would you think I'm married to Tara?"

Kendra sensed her face growing warm. "You have the same last name. You live in the same building."

He waited until he regained his composure. "This is great! This is wonderful! Wait until she hears you thought… Kendra, Tara is my sister. Yes, we live in the same building, but different apartments."

In the space of a second, she felt her face go from warm to hot enough to fry an egg, which would certainly be appropriate. Her hands shot up to cover it.

Ohmygod! What have I done? What he must think of me now!

"Kendra." His voice penetrated her mortification and racing thoughts. "Please, look at me."

Slowly her hands dropped, but she couldn't bring herself to meet his eyes.

"Kendra, I can see how you might have assumed that, given how we behaved together in the store that day. But it just never occurred to me that…if it had, I would have said something. Come on, don't be embarrassed. It was an honest mistake."

She raised her eyes and saw concern mixed with amusement in his eyes.

"Can you imagine how stupid I feel right now?"

"Actually, I can. It involved a certain professor of mine in college. And if you let me take you to dinner tonight, I'll tell you all about it."

"Really?"

He nodded and held up his right hand. "Scout's honor."

"I'll need a few minutes to get changed."

"Take all the time you need. I'll lock up for you."

Just before she vanished through the curtain, he

added, "But do me a favor, please."

"What?"

"Tonight, leave off the beard."

~ ~ ~ ~ ~ ~

Thank you for reading *Beginnings*. I hope you enjoyed the stories and will stop by Amazon to write a quick review and let me and others know what you thought. If you do, please include which Beginning you liked best.

Please turn the page to find a **Bonus Beginning**, the opening chapter of *Coffee in Common*, the story of a group of young Bostonians during the most incredible, life-altering month of their lives, a month of revelations and challenges in which new friendships are formed, new loves are found, and old loves are renewed.

Thanks again!

Dee Mann

Bonus Beginning

Coffee in Common

WEDNESDAY, MAY 5, 2004

7:40 AM

Paul DiLorenzo and Roberto Tello stood in line at Coffey's Coffee as they did nearly every workday morning. It wasn't unusual to find the line of customers snaking around inside the shop and then stretching out the door, even on the blustery, frigid mornings that frequently passed for spring in New England.

There were no lattés, or double mocha cappuccinos to be found at Coffey's. Seventy-two year old Gil Coffey didn't believe in trendy. For forty-nine years he'd been serving hand-made-on-the-premises pastry and bagels and the very best caffeine fix in downtown Boston, and didn't see any reason to change.

Rumor had it that representatives of some large chains periodically bought Coffey's coffee, not to drink, but to analyze in an attempt to determine what made it so good. So far, they'd not succeeded.

In 1994, when Starbucks moved into the area, one of Gil's employees took a marker to her name badge and became Barista Betty. Gil and the customers thought it a hoot. At the time, most folk in the area still thought *barista* was Italian for *barkeeper*. So Gil had new badges made for all the employees, a practice that now, years later, had become tradition.

"...but there was no *way* he was going to strike him out."

Paul was only half paying attention to his friend as he silently debated the merits of ordering one of Gil's amazing blueberry muffins versus a cinnamon-raisin bagel with cream cheese.

"He hasn't struck him out in three years. So why in the hell would Francona leave him in there with the bases loaded?"

"Maybe he had a hunch." He watched Barista Akina bring three cups to the counter for the girl in front of them.

"No maybes. The guy needs his head examined. There's no way he should be managing a little league team much less the Red Sox."

Paul enjoyed baseball and the Red Sox, but Rob was one of those fanatical fans for whom Red Sox Nation was created.

Akina twisted the three cups into a cardboard carrier and asked the woman, "Will there be anything else today?"

"Whatever you're giving away for free," she said with a grin as she reached into her purse.

Paul was about to answer Rob, but instead whipped his head around and blurted out, "Hey, that's my line."

Her eyes met his when she turned to see who had shouted in her ear. "Excuse me?"

Paul could only stare, captivated by her dark brown eyes, the smoothness of her skin, the gentle slope of her nose, the whiteness of her teeth, and the way her lips seemed to make him ache. He sensed the color rising in his cheeks and felt his heart quicken, unsure if it was his embarrassment or her amazing eyes making him feel suddenly very strange and self-conscious.

Finally he managed, "I ah, I'm ah, sorry. I said, 'that's

my line.' I almost always say that when someone asks if I want anything else."

The woman's skeptical frown was followed by first one, then the other eyebrow arching to accentuate her disbelief. "You say 'that's my line' whenever someone asks if you want anything else?"

"No, no." He was so rattled he didn't realize she was joking. "I mean I always say *that*, what you said, when someone asks if I want anything else."

Her simple, "Really!" made it obvious she didn't believe him. He turned to Rob in desperation. "Tell her. Don't I always say that?"

Crap. That sounds so lame she must think I'm an idiot.

There was no longer any doubt his face burned from making a fool of himself.

Rob rolled his eyes and nodded as he turned to face the girl. "Yah, he does. He says that *all* the time."

The girl added a wrinkled brow.

Are these two working on a new pickup line or are they simply demented?

"See." Paul tried to look hopeful.

Akina cleared her throat. "That will be nine dollars and twenty-one cents please."

The woman turned back, removed a ten from her red leather wallet and handed it over. "Keep the change."

She dropped the wallet in her purse, picked up the tray, turned her head to smile briefly but dismissively at Paul and Rob, and headed for the door.

The two stepped up to the counter. Rob ordered his coffee and perused the display cases filled with rich, moist muffins, flaky, sweet pastry, and assorted giant bagels. Paul watched the girl until she walked through the front door.

No sooner had it closed behind her than he turned to

Rob, then back to the door, then back to Rob, who'd glanced over in time to catch his friend's brief ballet and knew what was coming. He broke for the door, calling back over his shoulder for Rob to get him the usual and that he'd meet him at the office.

Out on the street, he performed another dance, twisting left, then right, then left again, finally catching sight of her in the morning crowd. She was walking slowly, gracefully, and he could not help but admire the gentle curves of her very feminine form as he hurried to catch up. Her dark-auburn hair shone in the morning light, swinging back-and-forth across her shoulders in a gentle counterpoint to the sway of her softly rounded hips.

"Excuse me," he said, touching her lightly on the left shoulder.

She glanced back, then stopped and turned toward him, her face filled with curiosity.

Paul realized he had no idea what to say. Something was drawing him to this attractive stranger, but whatever it might be, it was not providing any dialogue.

"Hi. I'm Paul. I, ahh, well I couldn't let you go away without talking to you. I mean, I'm, well…"

What the hell is wrong with me?

The woman's curiosity morphed into mild amusement at his continued fumbling.

He took a deep breath, let it out, and shook his head, not wanting to believe he could be acting like such a dolt. He felt like he was fourteen again, facing Susie Quan, the girl who gave him his first lesson in rejection.

"Wait. Please, let me start again. I swear I'm not usually this much of a loser around women. My name's Paul. Paul DiLorenzo. And you are…?"

"Wondering how often you stop girls on the street to make yourself look foolish." Impatience mixed with the amusement in her eyes.

He grinned at her quickness. "Thankfully, this is the first, and please let it be the last, time."

As before, he found her eyes hypnotic, even though they were now almost laughing at him. He shrugged.

"I really don't make a habit of accosting women on the street. It's just that, back there in the coffee shop was the first time I've ever heard anyone else use that line. I've been saying it since I was a teenager and when I heard you, something sort of clicked. Then, when you turned and our eyes met, something clicked again. I know it sounds crazy, but as I watched you walk out the door, this feeling came over me that I had to come after you, that I had to get to know you or I'd miss out on someone…something really important."

"You mean, like, the universe or God or something was telling you to chase after me?"

Clearly confused, Paul replied, "Well…I don't know, but, yah, I guess."

The woman chuckled, shook her head, and asked, "Does this line usually work for you or are you trying out new material today?" Without waiting for a reply, she turned and resumed her slow stroll down the sidewalk.

She's blowing me off. Why the hell am I acting like this? What is it about this girl that has me so off-balance?

He hurried to catch up, desperate for a miracle, a way to salvage this mess.

"Wait. I mean, can I walk with you. Walk you to work or wherever you're going? I really don't ever do this…you know, approach someone on the street like this. But what I said back there was the truth. Please. I won't even ask your name. If you don't think I'm worth a chance by the time we get to your building, or wherever, I'll leave and you'll never see me again."

She paused and appeared to weigh his offer. Then, with a playful half-smile said, "Okay. It's a deal. You have until we get to my building. Go."

She started walking slowly again. Paul kept pace on her left, feeling hopeful again.

"As I said, I'm Paul DiLorenzo. I'm an associate editor at Davis Phillips publishers, and…" He turned his head to stare at her as they walked. "…I can't believe how attracted I am to you when I don't know a thing about you. My…"

They'd traveled about 30 feet when the woman stopped and turned to face him.

"Well, here we are," she said, interrupting him.

Huh?

He'd expected to have more time to make an impression.

"Thanks for walking me," she said as she started toward the office building behind him.

Completely crushed, Paul could only stand there, frozen and speechless.

A quick glance at his face as she passed startled her, but she continued toward the building. Shoulders slumped, Paul stared after her, a poster boy for total defeat.

She reached for the handle, pulled open the door, then turned and stared at him for almost twenty seconds, her gaze hard and appraising. Then her eyes softened and she said, "I usually have coffee at lunch, usually around 12:30." She started to turn away but glanced back again, smiling.

"And my name is Jillian."

10:01 AM

Davis Phillips Publishers, the nation's third largest producer of beautiful coffee-table books that no one ever reads, occupied the fifth floor of the nine-story O'Malley

Building on the corner of Tremont and Winter Streets, across from the northeast corner of the Boston Common and two blocks north of the Heritage Building into which Paul had watched Jillian vanish a few hours ago.

Paul shared an office with the three other members of his team, his best friend, Rob Tello, team leader Thomas Driscoll, and the recently hired Priya Kumar.

"Geez, I hate those meetings," Paul whined as he and Priya walked away from the conference room. "Sixty minutes of my life wasted. You'd think…ah, who cares. Let's go get coffee."

"Shouldn't we tell Tom, first?"

"Nah. He won't care, as long as we bring him some."

Passing by the company coffee room, they headed for the elevator. Neither saw any reason to drink brown sludge when Coffey's was only two minutes away.

The ride down had been silent, but as the elevator doors opened to the lobby, Priya asked, "Mind if I ask you a personal question?"

"I don't know. About what?"

"Rob."

"Priya, trust me, you don't want to go out with him. Besides he's…"

Her laughter echoed off the marble walls. "Lord, no. It took me about two minutes to figure him out. Besides, remember my first day?"

Paul grinned and nodded.

"I was just wondering how long you've been friends. It's pretty clear you knew each other before working here."

"Oh yah, we go back to high school. We were best friends. Played ball on the same teams, dated cheerleaders, did stupid stuff together.

"We sort of lost touch after high school. I was going to Tufts and he ended up at Florida State. Then just before the end of his freshman year, his dad landed a great job near where the Red Sox have spring training, so his parents moved south." He laughed. "While all the other kids were heading to party places for spring break, Rob was watching the Red Sox every day at training camp."

Priya shared the laugh. "I can see that. He does seem to like his baseball. So when did you connect again?"

"About three years ago, not long after I started here. This girl Jody in accounting brought him to the company Christmas party. I tell ya, Pri, it was like I'd just seen him the day before."

"That's the hallmark of a true friendship," she said, walking through the door Paul held open for her.

"I guess so," he agreed as they approached the end of the short line. "He was teaching high school English at the time but hated the politics and bullshit. So when his predecessor announced she'd be resigning when her baby was born, I got him to apply for the job." He laughed again. "I think a lot of women in the company rue the day he started."

"Why? He seems like such a nice guy."

"He is. But you've only known him since he started going out with Lisa. You wouldn't know it to look at him, but he's always been a wicked player. In high school, he developed this kind of…mystique, I guess, as a party animal and chick magnet. Girls seemed to find his personality and charm and sense of humor irresistible despite his looks. I probably shouldn't admit this, but the best part of being friends with him was the leftovers."

"Leftovers?"

Paul nodded, looking sheepish. "The friends of the girls he went out with, the ones he broke up with after a few weeks, you know what I mean?"

"You called them leftovers?" Offense blazed in her eyes, but he was saved from having to answer when

Barista Manny asked what he could get for them.

Four minutes later, as the door to Coffey's closed behind them, Priya punched his arm hard enough that he almost dropped the cardboard cup holder. "Leftovers! What is it with men and their need to objectify and demean?"

She stomped off, leaving him rubbing his arm as he hurried to catch up.

"Priya, I'm sorry. That's what we used to say in high school. We were stupid kids with too many hormones. Come on, don't be angry."

An hour later, Paul was still getting the silent treatment, much to the amusement of Rob and Tom.

Priya glanced at him.

I suppose I should let him off the hook. After all, it was a long time ago, and he is *such a gentleman now. And I guess I was really taking out on him all the crap from other guys.*

Tom clearing his throat drew her eyes across the office to the desk that faced hers. She took in his familiar round freckled face, bushy orange-red hair, and trim but stocky five-foot eleven-inch build.

He could change his name to Mahatma Chang or anything else and you would still know he was of Irish descent. Rob, on the other hand, has that everyman look. He really could come from manywheres.

Her eyes returned to Paul as she let her thoughts drift back to her first day at DPP.

* * *

Priya was very nervous. She had arrived early but stayed out of the way until all three guys were safely at their desks. Then she walked in, closed the door, placed her bag on her desk, lifted her arms over her head in a swimsuit pose, and said, smiling, "Good morning, guys. Let's see a show of hands. Who wants to see me naked?"

The men were stunned into silence. They stared, unblinking, unmoving, like clichéd deer transfixed by the bright headlights of an oncoming car. She stared back for a few seconds then started laughing as she pointed to each in turn and said, "Liar, liar, and liar."

Her laughter relaxed them a bit and Rob's hand inched up slowly until it was above his head.

"Ah," she said, "an honest man." Slowly, she shook her head from side-to-side, turned to face him and said, "Rob, it will never happen. Ever." Her hands moved to indicate her attractive, but conservative business suit. "This is as close as you will ever get to seeing heaven."

Shoot. That sounded awfully conceited.

"Look guys, I had to leave two really good jobs in the past year because the men I worked with either wouldn't take me seriously or couldn't keep their eyes, and other parts, to themselves. I'm good at what I do, and this seems like a really nice, friendly place, but I came here to work, and that's all I came here to do. If that's going to be a problem, please tell me now before I get comfortable in the job."

Her new coworkers were grinning broadly. Tom stood and gave her a slight bow of appreciation. "Well done, ma'am. Well done."

* * *

In the three months since then, she'd never once caught any of them looking at her in anything but a friendly and professional way. Even when the office banter turned suggestive, or even sexual, she was just one of the team.

She sighed, decided it was time to forgive Paul, and tossed a paperclip at him to get his attention. "So what happened with the girl this morning? Did you get lucky?"

Paul grinned, happy things were back to normal, then glared at Rob. "I should have figured you'd start blabbing the minute you got here." He turned his attention back to Tom and Priya. "To answer your question…oh yeah…I was on my game."

"Sure you were," Rob jeered, remembering his performance in the coffee shop. "Did you get her number?"

"Number, ha! Who needs a number?"

"He struck out," Priya said. "He got nothing and now he'll be getting nothing. Poor Paul."

Tom snorted his agreement, holding up his right hand with thumb and forefinger forming an 'L'.

"Lady, gentlemen, please. You forget to whom you are speaking. I was so smooth, so charming, *so* damned irresistible that I didn't even ask for her number.

"See, I told you…" Priya began.

"But," Paul continued, interrupting her. "I did make a date for lunch today."

11:30 AM

11:30! How could it only be 11:30?

Paul hadn't been this anxious for lunchtime to arrive since high school, when he'd skip the entrée in the cafeteria and head right outside to meet Sue Ellen for a little lip-locking dessert.

He studied Rob, sitting at this desk across the room, engrossed in whatever he was editing.

I wonder if he remembers the night we went to the Sheepfold with Suzy and...what was her name...the redhead with the big boobs...and he got out of the car in his boxers to take a whiz and...what the hell *is her name...convinced Suzy to drive off toward the entrance as if we were going to leave him there. Man, I can still hear us all laughing, still see him running across the parking lot by moonlight, cursing and pleading.*

As he forced it from his face, he was glad none of his co-workers had caught his evil grin.

Hmmm...did I ever thank him for introducing me to Suzy?

His gaze drifted right to Priya.

She really looks hot today...I wonder if she has a boyfriend. She must. Probably some muscle-bound face with a big dick. Girls like her can get anyone they want. But she never talks about dating anyone...and she doesn't seem like the superficial type...unless she's a great actress...but that stunt she pulled the first day...no way...she's okay. Just private, I guess. I wonder if Jillian will really show up...damn, what the hell was wrong with me this morning...must have been those eyes...great eyes...maybe she...

Tom's voice rang out. "Hey, DiLorenzo, you working or dreaming over there?"

12:15 PM

Jillian hurried toward the coffee shop. A curious anxiety nibbled at the back of her mind. She wanted to be there before he arrived but wasn't sure why. The wind blew her hair around and though she tried to keep it in place, she knew she'd need to fix it once inside.

The lunchtime crowd, like the wind, all seemed to be coming toward her, making it difficult to move quickly. As she drew closer to the shop, she realized she was actually nervous about meeting this guy.

Paul DiLorenzo. Nice name. And he is kind of cute.

But he was so flustered this morning. Do I really want to sit through a whole lunch with some spaz? What would Liz say to do? Be cool. Just be cool and detached and make him work to impress me. But lord, that look on his face this morning. If it hadn't been for that look... Come on, girl, get a grip. You've shot down plenty of come-ons before. But that look...not just disappointment... almost...devastation. How can you not at least give a guy a chance when he's devastated at the thought of not seeing you again. And I guess it was *kind of sweet the way he was stumbling over himself to impress me. I never did* that *to a guy before.*

She reached the shop, pulled open the door and stepped inside. It felt good to get out of the wind.

Mmmm...it smells wonderful in here. Coffee mixed with the pastry...I sure wish someone would figure out how to capture it in a bottle, so I can spray it around the apartment.

She was standing a few feet inside the door and when it opened again, the cold air roused her from her reverie. With a contented sigh, she turned to find a table and saw Paul sitting at the one in the corner, his back to the front window. He was reading from a stack of papers and there were three or four cups on the table.

Damn.

She quickly finger-combed her hair.

How long has he been here? And what's with all the coffee? Are other people coming? Is this some kind of game after all? Maybe I should just get out of here before he sees me.

She hesitated, still trying to smooth out her hair but, without a mirror, not having much success.

What the hell...he takes me as I am or not at all.

She removed her scarf and started toward the table. Holding the scarf in her left hand, she used her right to unbutton her coat. When she was closer, she saw she was correct about the coffees. There were three sitting unopened in the center of the table and one, obviously his and already half empty, near the edge.

"Hi," she said with a neutral smile as she reached the table.

"Hi," he replied without thinking. Then he looked up and jumped out of his seat.

"Oh, hi!" he repeated, this time with genuine enthusiasm. "You're early."

"Not as early as you, I see."

Her eyes flicked to the table, then back to Paul. "Have you been working?" She gestured reflexively and her scarf caught his cup, spilling the coffee all over the papers.

When they heard the cup go over, they looked down at the mess and simultaneously groaned, "Oh crap!"

Their heads snapped back up at the matching exclamations as all through the shop, heads turned to see what was happening.

Jillian was mortified. "I am *so* sorry. I…"

"That's okay," he said, interrupting, as he grabbed the few napkins on the table and started blotting at the drenched manuscript. "Just…can you get me some more napkins?"

He continued to blot at the spilled coffee but it was futile now. The napkins were saturated. Jillian hurried off, trying to ignore the stares from other customers, and returned with a napkin dispenser. She pulled out three small napkins which emptied the dispenser. Quickly, she turned it around to find the other side empty as well.

"I don't believe this," she moaned, silently cursing her decision to stay.

She hurried off again to return with two handfuls of napkins. Dropping them all over the spill, she began sopping up the coffee, so embarrassed that she couldn't look at him.

"I really am *so* sorry. I can't believe I did that. I've probably ruined your work and now…now…"

She wadded up a pile of saturated napkins, still not able to meet his eyes.

"…I…I'm sorry. I should go. Really, I'm sorry."

She turned to leave.

"Wait! Where are you going? You just got here."

Paul finished mopping up the coffee and piled the wet napkins on the edge of table against the wall.

"Please, calm down. Didn't your mom ever tell you not to cry over spilled coffee. Or was that milk. No matter. Come on, sit down. It's okay."

He could see how embarrassed she was. Gently he said, "Really, Jillian. No harm done."

He moved to the other side of the table and pulled out the chair for her.

Jillian forced herself to face him and saw he was grinning.

He rattled the chair a bit, his eyes pleading with her to stay. "Please?"

She forced a weak smile and took the offered seat. As he moved back to his chair, she shrugged off her jacket and nervously ran her fingers through her hair again, suddenly hoping it didn't look too horrible. They stared at each other for a few moments, neither one really sure what to say. Then Paul started to chuckle. He tried his best to contain it but couldn't and a full-fledged laugh burst through.

His laughter was infectious. Jillian noticed her mood growing lighter as the corners of her mouth curled into a smile.

He is so strange!

"What's so funny?"

Paul took a few seconds to get the laughter under control. As he did, she again took in his thick, brown hair with its reddish highlights, his brown eyes flecked with gold, his straight nose, and his full, laughing lips. She remembered from this morning that he carried himself with a casual straightness. She noticed he sat that way, too. His shoulders were not exceptionally broad, nor his arms particularly muscular, yet he seemed to exude a quiet physical prowess.

"Well, think about it. Our first meeting this morning was somewhat of a disaster, with me acting unbelievably foolish. And now our second meeting starts with another, ah…small blip. But this time it's you who…"

He started laughing again, quietly this time, enjoying the irony of the situation. Jillian started to say something but he stopped her.

"Wait, please. Before you say anything else, before anything else happens…what is your last name?"

Somehow, that simple question relaxed her and Jillian grinned at his urgency.

"Marshall. Jillian Marshall."

Paul started to extend his hand over the table to shake hands but retreated a bit and hooked it around the coffee cups.

Jillian feigned indignation and extended her hand straight over the them. As their hands approached, a small jolt of static electricity made them both jump. Startled, each wondered if the spark was an omen and, if so, what sort. Then, as they shook hands, a spark of a different sort passed between them.

"Paul DiLorenzo," he said. "I am *really* happy to meet you Ms. Jillian Marshall."

"And I'm still a little embarrassed, but happy to meet you, too. I hope I didn't destroy anything really important."

Paul picked up one of the wet sheets of paper.

"No, don't worry about it. It's just the only copy of a recently discovered manuscript by Ernest Hemingway. It'll dry." He paused, looking worried. "I hope."

Jillian's wide-eyed stare vanished when she saw him grin again.

"Jerk. I almost believed you for a second."

"Sorry. I couldn't resist. How long do you have for lunch?"

"I should be back by one."

Paul nodded slightly. "Me too." He paused for a deep breath. "You know, I probably shouldn't ever bring this up again, but I really am sorry I was so clumsy this morning about meeting you. I'm usually a fairly articulate guy."

"That's okay. You were nervous. Nervous can be kind of cute. And let's be honest here, your clumsy this morning doesn't come close to my clumsy a few minutes ago."

"Okay then, we're even. I hope you won't mind me saying this so soon, but you are the second most beautiful woman I've ever seen in person."

Jillian blushed, pleased and flattered by the compliment.

"Come on, I know I'm not a beast, but the second…"

"No, really. You are definitely the second most beautiful woman I've ever met.

Her blush deepened.

"Okay, but just the second? Who's the first?"

Paul looked right into her shining, beautiful brown eyes and said. "Everyone else."

Stunned at the unexpected reply, Jillian stared at him for a second before she burst out laughing.

"You really are a jerk. I owe you big time for that."

Looking pleased and a little relieved, Paul glanced up to thank God she was laughing.

"I'm sorry. I couldn't stop myself. And I figured that if I'm on trial, I might as well let you see who I really am. If you hadn't laughed just then, well, I'd have been heartbroken, but I'd have known we'd never really get along."

"What do you mean 'on trial'?"

"Didn't you come here to decide whether you liked me enough to give me your number and try me out on a real date?"

Jillian looked as if she were about to protest, but Paul continued on.

"That's okay. That's what you should be doing when a strange guy embarrasses himself on the street. I mean, anyone can act like a fool for a few minutes in order to charm a beautiful girl, but it takes a special kind of guy to sustain it for a whole lunch. And you don't strike me as the type of girl who would waste much time on that kind of guy."

"And how *do* I strike you?"

"Right through the heart, so far."

Jillian's blush had faded, but rose anew at this latest compliment. Desperate to change the subject, she nodded toward the three cups.

"Are these all for me?"

"Yes."

"*Three* coffees?"

"Well, I didn't know how you liked your coffee, but I figured one of the three you bought this morning had to be for you, so I talked to Akina and…"

"Akina?"

"The barista who waited on you this morning."

"You're on a first name basis with the people here?"

"Not really, just Akina, and only since noon when I got here. I took a chance she might remember you, which she did, since you come in all the time with the same order. Or so she said. So I asked her for the same three coffees and here they are."

Pointing to them one-by-one, he said, "Decaf regular, black two sugars, and milk dark no sugar."

Jillian started to reach for one but Paul stopped her. "Wait. Let me guess."

He studied her for a few seconds, then picked up the milk-dark-no sugar and handed it to her with a hopeful look on his face.

"I'm impressed. How did you know?"

"I didn't. I guessed. Or rather, I hoped."

"Hoped?"

"Uh-huh. That's how I take mine."

Her disbelief was unmistakable.

"Really! I told you this morning I had a strange feeling when I first saw you. It was like I knew you, even though I didn't know you. It…but this is all getting a little too heavy."

Paul picked up his empty cup. "How about sharing some of that coffee?"

Jillian poured half of the coffee from her cup into his, then handed it back.

"I don't think it's hot anymore," she said.

"That's okay. I'm used to cold coffee. Besides, just looking at you will keep me warm."

"Oh *please*," she muttered, rolling her eyes.

Paul laughed. "Okay, I guess I *am* laying it on a little thick." He checked his watch and realized time was getting short. "As much as I'd like to sit here with you all afternoon, we only have about twenty-five minutes left before you have to decide and all you know about me is how I like my coffee, that I can act goofy, and that I have a strange sense of humor."

He locked eyes with her, his gaze never wavering as he continued.

"So fire away. Ask me anything you want to know. Job, school, shoe size, favorite Backstreet Boy. Anything. Because when I walk out that door in a little while…" He reached across the table to move a tuft of hair away from her eye. The touch of his finger against her skin sent another spark through her, a warm, welcome spark. "…I'll either have your phone number, or a huge hole where my heart used to be."

6:20 PM

Jillian closed the door to her apartment, dropped her keys in her purse, shrugged off her coat, and hung both on the wooden pegs on the wall next to the door. The scarf she held up, smiling with the memory of the chaos it caused.

It had been a long, eventful day both in and out of work, but she was still full of energy. Happy and excited her lunch with Paul had gone so well after its disastrous beginning, she was dying to tell her friends all the details. But it was still too early. Neither Liz nor Jenna would be home from work for at least fifteen minutes.

The golden glow of the afternoon sun streamed through the four oversized, Victorian-era double-hung wood sash windows that formed a bay overlooking the street. It cast curious shadows in the two alcoves, one that held her bed, nightstand, and dresser, and the other, an efficiency kitchen.

She took the big feather duster from the umbrella stand by the door and moved around the room dusting the photos, prints, and posters that brightened the room and, even on a gloomy day, made visitors feel welcome. Then she fixed the pillows on the floral print sofa and two overstuffed chairs that reminded her of the wallpaper in her room as a child, all the while, thinking of him.

Suddenly in the mood for music, she loaded her special mix CD into the player.

Always and forever
Each moment with you
Is just like a dream to me
That somehow came true, yeah

The sweet sound of Luther Vandross filled the apartment. Her eyelids drooped, half closed as she conjured an image of Paul smiling at her the way he did when he was holding the chair for her, urging her to stay. Something about him, even the thought of him, made her feel strangely comfortable. He'd been so nice, so easy to talk to once she was past the humiliation of spilling coffee on his work.

She grinned, remembering the exasperation on his face as he tried to sop up half a cup of coffee with a few small napkins. Then her face softened, almost glowed, as she remembered the light in his eyes when he'd moved that wisp of hair and said those sweet things.

Lost in her fantasy, she ambled to the windows to close the curtains, flopped on the sofa, then almost immediately jumped up and headed for the kitchen where she grabbed a bottle from the fridge. Sipping the water, still swaying with the music, she strolled to the bedroom alcove and sat on the edge of the bed, recalling yet again the events of the day. The last strains of the song faded and were replaced by another Vandross standard, *Here & Now*. She giggled out loud at the memory of how goofy and desperate he'd been when they first met, but was startled out of her reverie by the shrill ring of the phone.

Hoping it would be him, but knowing it was probably some telemarketer, she screwed the cap back on the bottle and rolled backward over the bed to grab the cordless phone on the nightstand.

"Hello?"

"You forgot to take your cell phone off silent again. It's a wonder you have any friends at all since you make it so hard for people to reach you."

"Hi, Liz." She tried to keep her excitement out of her voice. "You're home early!"

"Jenna and I both got out early. I just talked with her. We were thinking about Piazolla's for dinner tonight. Lucy from work said she was there twice last week and there were lots of mighty fine guys hanging and…"

Unable to contain herself, Jillian blurted out, "Liz, stop. I have to tell you something. You won't believe what happened to me today."

Elizabeth could hear the particular excitement in her friend's voice and knew only one thing could have put it there.

"Don't even tell me his name. I promised Jenna I'd pick her up in ten minutes and if you start talking now she'll be waiting on me for an hour. We'll be over as fast as we can get through traffic. And forget about Piazolla's tonight."

"Okay, okay. But you and Jenna hurry. And bring Thai."

7:10 PM

DHL sat on the corner of Charles and Chestnut Streets, two blocks north of the Boston Common. Named for the writer D.H. Lawrence when it first opened three decades ago, it had quickly become a trendy, English-pub-style watering hole. Today, it attracted a loyal clientele who were more interested in a relaxed atmosphere than being seen in the vicinity of whomever happened to be hot at the moment.

Paul and Rob liked DHL because it was never so crowded or loud you couldn't carry on a conversation. That the place offered thirty-six beers and ales on tap, with another three dozen in bottles didn't hurt much either.

"Your favorite Backstreet Boy? You didn't really say that?" Rob's incredulous stare conveyed more than his words.

Paul surveyed the long mahogany and brass bar that ran along the left wall and the lacquered pine tables surrounded by wood chairs comfortably padded with dark, leather cushions that filled most of the rest of the space. "I swear. It just came out. And I can't figure out why. I never even liked the Backstreet Boys." He shook his head. "But it didn't matter. We hit it off, man. We really hit it off. She was so uptight and embarrassed after spilling my coffee but then she just seemed to relax. And after that, there were no games, no posturing. We were just talking and laughing. Really connecting."

Rob screwed his face into a grimace. "Geez, man, you realize you're starting to sound like a girl."

"Up yours. Are you telling me you and Lisa never talked about stuff?" He knew Rob had suggested drinks for a reason and figured it was time to start the poking and prodding.

In response to silence, Paul said, "Look, buddy. I really didn't want to come here tonight. I wanted to head home and call Jillian. If you hadn't practically begged me…you know?"

Rob sighed. "Well, yah, of course. We talked about movies, and food, and sex, and things to do. Stuff like that."

"Maybe that was the problem. Maybe she wanted to talk about more than that. Feelings and stuff. Chick stuff, you know?"

Rob stared into space for a few seconds then sighed, nodding slightly. "Yah, maybe."

"So what's going on there?"

"Same as yesterday. Same as last week. We're on a break. She wanted a break to think about us."

He paused for a few seconds, again shaking his head. "What's there to think about? We go out, we have fun, the sex is great." He grimaced. "It's her friends, I know it's her friends. They don't like me much. They think I'm a troll."

Caught off-guard, Paul almost choked on his beer as he tried hard not to laugh. "A troll?"

"They don't think I'm handsome enough for her. They want her to find some guy who's more in her league. I'm too ordinary for them, which would be okay if I had lots of money, but I don't. I guess I embarrass them. When all the beautiful folk get together they don't want to have to look at commoners."

"Come on, Rob. Lisa is *not* that shallow. She…"

"I know, I know. But her friends are. And they're at her all the time about me."

"How do you know? You've heard them?"

Rob fidgeted with discomfort. "Two months ago we were at a party. It was a benefit thing for some beavers or possums or something like that. Anyway, I'm standing at the bar waiting for our drinks. Lisa's off with some museum people she knows. These two girls come up behind me talking."

* * *

"So how long has she been seeing him?" Kiki asked.

"Like, a couple of months," her friend Rachel replied. "I can't believe you didn't hear."

"How would I hear? Four months I'm in Paris and did anyone call me? *You* didn't call me."

"Yes I did. Two weeks after you left. You said you were having *trÃ¨s* much fun and met this guy FranÃ§ois, and just *didn't* have time to talk because he was waiting for you in the lobby and…"

"Oh…well…yes, now I remember. Well…"

"I decided you'd call if you got lonely. Not that I could imagine you *getting* lonely in a country full of hot guys."

"Girl, you can not imagine. But that's for another day. So you say she's been seeing him for two months?"

Rachel nodded. "Two or three."

"But why? Does he have this enormous package or something? Or is he, like, really rich? He certainly doesn't dress it if he is."

"I don't know about his package, but he can't have much money. Nobody ever heard of him." She shrugged. "None of us can figure it out."

"Has anyone asked her?"

Rachel didn't even try to hide her disdain. "Of course," she said, then added in a mocking tone, "She said he treats her nice and makes her laugh."

"And that's supposed to make up for his looking like a truck driver? What *is* Lisa thinking?"

Rob didn't usually listen to chatter or gossip but his ears perked up when he heard Lisa's name. He paid close attention now, as the women continued their conversation.

"I don't know. But she's, like, totally into this guy. Everyone keeps telling her she should dump him and find someone in her own league, you know, because this guy is just so far beneath her. Oh, and you haven't heard the worst yet."

"What could be worse than no money and no looks?

"His name's Roberto something. I think he's from Mexico, or Puerto Rico, or someplace like that."

"No!"

"Yes!" Rob's voice mocked her exclamation.

The bartender had just placed the drinks on the bar. Rob grabbed one in each hand, turned, and smiled at the women.

"Actually, my family is from Ecuador."

Smiling, he introduced himself. "Roberto Tello. It's *so* nice to meet you. It's good to know Lisa has such warm, caring friends who look out for her best interests even when she's so obviously out of her mind."

Both girls were embarrassed to discover the subject of their gossip had overheard them, but neither appeared contrite. Just the opposite.

"Well, I'm sorry you heard that," Rachel sniffed, "but maybe it was for the best. You have to know that you're just a fling for her." She smiled viciously. "I mean, we all go slumming once in a while."

"Really? We all do that?"

"Those of us who, well, you know."

"Yes, I think I do know."

Not to be left out, Kiki chimed in. "You really should, you know, save yourself a lot of future pain and move on to someone who's more your type. I mean, this thing with you and her can't last. She'll get tired of people making fun of her because of you."

Rob's smile disappeared. Worry lines creased his forehead. "People, her friends you mean, make fun of her because she goes out with me?"

"Yes! All the time!" Her voice lowered as she confided, "You know, people at our level can be, well, mean sometimes."

"No!" Rob appeared confused. "I haven't noticed that at all since we've been together."

"Oh you wouldn't. I mean, we're not uncouth or anything. No one would come right out and say anything if you or she were, like, around. But people do talk and the talk certainly gets back to Lisa."

"Yes, I can imagine." He could no longer hide his contempt. "I guess it *is* a good thing she has friends like you two who she can count on to keep her abreast of all the mean and hurtful gossip your little minds produce."

Being chastised by someone she considered beneath her was unthinkable and Rachel's glare could have melted steel. "Sure, as if you never say anything about anyone. See, that's what I mean. You think you're as good as she is but you're not. Lisa should have someone who's her equal. Both socially and, ah, visually. You are not that person. And you'll never *be* that person."

Rob was growing tired of the two snobs, but his honor had been offended, something he could not let pass.

"Well…this was very enlightening. Very enlightening indeed. If you'll excuse me."

He started to walk between them, but appeared to stumble, sending the contents of one of the glasses spilling down the front of Rachel's dress. "Oh my. I'm so sorry. How clumsy of me."

Rachel was livid. "You did that on purpose. You…"

Rob interrupted her. "Please, let me get something to dry you off."

He turned to Kiki and said, "Here, hold this, while I get a towel."

He handed her the drink, which slipped from his fingers, bounced off her hand, and spilled on the front of *her* dress.

Kiki gave a short scream of dismay.

"Oh dear!" Rob said. "Again! I really *am* sorry." He turned to the bartender, who winked at him. "May I have some towels please?"

Both women were beside themselves now with fury. They could not believe any man, especially one like him, would treat them this way.

"You asshole!" Rachel seethed, her voice dripping with venom. "You stay away from us. Just remember, Lisa *will* dump you. And I'll be standing next to her laughing at you when she does."

* * *

Paul's raucous laughter caused a few heads to turn their way. "Are you serious? They really said that stuff? You really did that to both of them? Why did I never hear about this?"

"They did, and I did. When I told Lisa what happened, she couldn't believe I'd actually do something like that."

"I can understand. I'm having trouble believing it myself."

"Well, she insisted I promise never to do that to anyone again, no matter what the provocation, and not to tell anyone else about it." Rob shrugged. "You know Lisa. What else could I do but promise?"

Paul was still chuckling.

"I guess I see why you think her friends may have had something to do with it. All I can say is, I wish I had been there to see it."

Paul extended his hand, palm open and they exchanged slaps twice.

"Do you have to hang around a lot with these people?"

"No, not really. They're not friends like we're friends. Not any more. They're the kids of people in her parent's social circle. They all used to hang out when they were in high school, and I guess many of them still do, but Lisa doesn't really see them much…once in a while at some social thing."

"That would be once in a while too much for me."

"Me, too. But Lisa feels like she has to be friendly for her parents' sake."

"So, you haven't heard from her at all?"

"Not a word. And it's been, like, almost two weeks now. I called a couple of times but got her voice mail. I left a message once, but she never called me back."

"That's tough, dude."

"Yah, well, she said she wanted time alone to think, so I probably shouldn't be surprised. But I miss her, man, you know? We were so good together. I loved how proper she was in public and how wild she could be when we were alone."

He glanced away for a few seconds, trying to gauge whether to risk ridicule by continuing.

Paul read the indecision on his friend's face. "I know what you mean, buddy. It's like a big hole, a big empty place she used to fill, but now…nothing."

"Exactly." He decided to take the risk. "You know when you were talking about coffee girl before, and you said that when you saw her the first time you felt something click. Well, that's what happened to me when I first met Lisa."

"Did you ever tell her?"

"Tell her? No. I don't think I ever really acknowledged it to myself, much less to her. I mean, you know me. I've always been free, having a good time, one girl after another. Do you realize I'd been with Lisa for over five months before this break. Five months! That's the longest I've been with one girl since high school. Even then, I wasn't really exclusive with anyone. But with Lisa, it's different." He sighed. "You know, I realized last week that since I've been with her, I never even think about other women."

Paul looked skeptical. "Man, I've seen you ogling…"

"Yah, yah, I know. I look at pretty girls. But it's the

damnedest thing. I look, but I never fantasize about what it would be like to be with them anymore."

"Sounds like the 'L' word to me," Paul said. "Sounds like you have it bad. Did you ever tell her you loved her?"

"Of course, like when we were doing it and stuff."

"That's it?"

"What do you mean?"

Paul was shaking his head. "Rob, how can a man with Latino blood in his veins, a man who's had more women than most men dream of…how can you know so little about them? Are you seriously telling me you only told Lisa you loved her while you were screwing her?"

"No. Sometimes I'd tell her afterward, or before."

Rob was beginning to regret taking that chance. He wasn't comfortable talking about love and emotions. And he really didn't like talking about sex, although he'd engage in bragging banter with other guys when it seemed to be called for.

Paul noticed his friend withdrawing.

"Rob, Lisa is the steadiest, most unassuming girl I've ever met. She's smart, funny, looks great but doesn't seem to care, and, well, you know I could go on and on. Five months ago, for whatever reason I'll never know, she chose you. And until this taking-a-break thing, I thought you two were made for each other. So did everyone else, which is why none of us can figure out what the taking-a-break is all about.

"But now I think I understand. You believe it was her friends dissing you, but from what you say, they'd been doing that right along. No, this is not the fault of her friends, buddy, it's all your fault."

Paul took a swig of his beer, sat back, and waited for a reaction.

Rob looked dazed. After a minute he mumbled, "My fault?"

"Your fault," Paul shot back. "Man, if you want to keep a woman like Lisa you have to work at it. She can have any guy she wants in this town. Hell, she can probably have any guy she wants in the world. But she chose you. Why would she do that?"

"She said I made her laugh, and that I'm nice to her."

"Okay, that's what hooked her, but what kept her coming back for five months?"

"I don't know," Rob replied. "Good times, great sex?"

Paul signaled the bartender to send over another round.

"Rob, she can get that anywhere, and probably in greater quantity and quality."

"Hey…"

"Yah, blah, blah, I know. I've seen you in the shower, buddy. You ain't that special. Look, Lisa saw something in you, something that made her want to stick around. But you never gave her any reason to do so. Women want, no, they need to be told, to be reassured all the time. They need to hear the words, and not just when you're in bed with them. I'd bet money Lisa's trying to decide if you'll ever wake up and realize that being together involves more than fun and games, especially if she's thinking long term. You know what I mean about long-term?"

Rob nodded. "Yah, I guess so. But it's too late now. I can feel it. If she hasn't called in two weeks, she's not going to. Not until she gets up the nerve to tell me it's over for good."

"You don't know that."

"Yes I do."

"No, you don't. But what have *you* done the past two weeks to help her decide? You've done nothing but leave one message on her machine. What do you think that's telling her? It's telling her you don't care enough to pursue her."

"She said she didn't want to talk to me, she wanted the time alone."

"Bullshit. She wants you to come after her, to show her that you really want her, and not just for sex and smartass. She's waiting for you to decide if you really want her for the long haul. She's waiting for you to *do* something, you dope."

"Do what? What can I do?"

"What can you do? Are you serious? Send her flowers, call her and tell her how much you miss her. And leave that message if she doesn't answer the phone. Camp out on her door step. Invite her out to talk. Tell her you love her, stupid."

Paul punched Rob in the arm. "Tell her and *show* her how much you love her."

7:35 PM

Jillian opened her door and waited for her friends to hike up the twenty-one stairs to her floor.

She'd spent the forty-five minutes between hanging up with Liz and her friends' arrival vacuuming her already clean rugs, washing and polishing her already spotless bathroom fixtures, and setting dishes, glasses, and chopsticks on the burled oak coffee table she'd rescued from the trash last year and had spent an entire weekend restoring to beauty. It rested in front of the sofa which was nestled in the large window bay.

The girls bounced up the stairs whispering to each other, then hurried down the short hall when they noticed her waiting for them.

"Jilli's got a boyfriend, Jilli's got a boyfriend," Jenna sang as she pranced through the door and hung her jacket on a peg. "Liz and I discussed it on the way over and we decided we really don't want to know anything about him.

We'd rather watch a movie."

Liz nodded her agreement as she set the bag full of aromatic Thai food on the bar separating the kitchen from the rest of the studio.

"Oh, well, if you really don't want to hear about him…"

Just then, the CD Jillian had started earlier played the last chords of *I Believe In You And Me* and restarted with *Always and Forever*. The dreamy expression returned as her eyes slowly closed, and she began swaying slightly with the music, her thoughts suddenly far from friends and food.

Liz and Jenna exchanged astonished stares. Jillian was the practical one, not usually given to overly romantic flights of fancy. They watched her for a minute, grinning and pointing, mouthing silent questions and replies to each other.

"Okay," Jenna said, no longer able to keep silent. "Enough of this game. Anyone who can make her do *that* I *have* to hear about."

7:45 PM

Halfway through their third beer, the two had pretty much talked-out the Lisa situation. They'd been sitting quietly for a few minutes, each lost in his own thoughts.

Paul glanced at his watch, ready to split.

Man, I hate leaving him here like this, but I really want to get home and call Jillian. Why the hell is he just sitting there? I'd have been out of here long ago looking for her. It's like he really doesn't think he can do anything. But how can he not at least try?

He was about to tell Rob it was time to go when he noticed two women walk in. The shorter one waved their way as they approached the table.

"Hi Rob. Sorry we're late. We took the train and something happened and we sat there, stopped, for almost twenty minutes."

She leaned over to give Rob a short kiss. Perplexed, Paul's glare demanded to know what was going on.

"Hey, Debbie." He turned to the other girl. "You must be Marianne." When she nodded, he said, "Hi, I'm Rob and this is Paul."

"Pleased to meet you both." Forcing the glare from his face, Paul rose to shake their hands.

Introductions completed, Debbie said, "Pardon us for a minute. We need to find the little girls room."

The glare returned and as soon as the girls were out of earshot, he blasted Rob. "What the fuck is this? Did you set me up or something and not bother to ask me?"

"Take it easy, man. Debbie said her friend was staying with her for a few days and asked if I could find her a date for the evening. She wasn't even sure Marianne would want to come out, so I didn't say anything in case she didn't show. I didn't want to get your hopes up, you know?"

"Get my hopes up? Are you kidding? What if I already had a date tonight?"

"But you don't."

"But *you* didn't know that. Besides, I'm not interested in a date tonight. I want to go home and call Jillian."

"Who?"

"Jillian. Focus, Rob. The girl from the coffee shop. The girl I've been talking about all day. And who's Debbie?"

"I met her yesterday at the gym. If you think she looks good now, you should see her in spandex."

Paul's head moved slowly from side to side, unbelieving.

"And what about Lisa? You just finished telling me

how much you love her, how much you miss her, how you never think of other girls, and now you're ready to date this Debbie? Was that a joke? What if she sees you with her?"

"Hey, she's the one who wanted to take a break. Am I supposed to sit around and wait for her to make up her mind?"

"I don't believe this. Did you hear *anything* I said before? I told you to go after her, to convince her she wants you back. Do you think going out with someone else will accomplish that?"

"I don't know."

"Man, I really don't want to spend the night with…oh shit, here they come."

Rob glanced over his shoulder as girls emerged from the ladies room.

"Come on, man, be a friend. Be nice to her for a few hours so me and Debbie can get to know each other. I'll owe you one."

"A big one."

"A big one what?" Debbie asked.

Paul raised his hand and wiggled his little finger. "We were discussing Rob's desire to find a way to overcome his, ah, shortcoming."

7:55 PM

Laughter rang through the room. Jillian, Liz, and Jenna were sitting on the sofa. The table in front of them was littered with open take-out containers and water bottles.

"I'm telling you, he was so goofy and cute and he was trying so hard, but I really thought it was some kind of totally bad pick-up thing, you know?"

Liz and Jenna nodded.

"So my evil twin took over and I was *so* mean to him. But then, when I saw his face as I passed him, I started thinking maybe it wasn't just a line. So I let him know where I'd be for lunch and he, umm, he looked like he'd won the lottery."

"The lottery?" Jenna asked.

"Uh-huh, all happy and excited. I spent all morning debating if I should really go, you know. I mean, he could have been a good actor or some weirdo, but I went."

Jillian's eyes closed as she smiled again.

Liz grinned. "Jeez, she's at it again." She poked Jillian's arm. "Come on girl, snap out of it."

Jillian made a face but resumed her recitation. She reported everything that happened at lunch. Her friends interrupted frequently with questions, for clarifications, and to laugh out loud. They analyzed every sentence, every word, every inflection, gesture, raised eyebrow, scratched ear, and twitch of the lunchtime conversation. They chewed it all up and spit out every possible shade of meaning of every minute point until there was simply nothing left to scrutinize.

"So how ugly is he?" Liz asked.

"What do you mean?"

"Well, so far, we've heard how goofy he was and then how charming he was and blah, blah, blah, but not a word about how he looks. What's the matter with him?"

"I already told you he was cute."

"No you didn't," Jenna said. "You said he *acted* goofy and cute."

"Well my mistake. I'll tell you…" Jillian took several long sips from her water bottle before checking the various containers to see what morsels might remain. Then she said, "You know, I really should go pee. I'll be back in a minute."

Liz grabbed her left arm. "You're going nowhere."

She motioned for Jenna to hold her right.

"Yah," Jenna said. "Pee your pants if you have to but you're not getting up until we know what he looks like."

Jillian pretended to struggle for a few seconds, until all three were laughing again.

"He is sooo cute. He's about five-ten, has brown hair, cut short, and these incredible brown eyes that seemed to see right inside me. He's thin, but not skinny and has a really nice smile with a dimple right here." Jillian pointed to a spot on her left cheek a little less than an inch away from the corner of her mouth. "Satisfied?"

"He sounds really great," Jenna told her. "Is he cuter than Aiden?"

Jillian flinched. Liz glared at Jenna, who just shrugged.

"I'm sorry. It's been so long I didn't think his name was still verboten."

"Well, it is," Liz barked. "And you should…"

Jillian laid a hand on her friend's arm. "It's okay, Liz, it just caught me off-guard." But her dreamy smile had vanished. She turned to Jenna. "Neither one is cuter, really. They're too different to compare like that. Paul has a kind of Mediterranean look while…the other one had that blond, Nordic thing going."

Jenna nodded. "I remember."

"But when's he supposed to call?" Liz asked, to change the subject.

"I don't know," Jillian replied, as her smile returned. "I was hoping he'd call tonight. He said he would, but it's after eight already so maybe not."

"Could be he had to work late." Jenna said.

"Or had a date," Liz teased.

"Maybe." Jillian shrugged. "I'm not worrying about it. If he calls, he calls. If he doesn't, he doesn't." She jumped up from the sofa and headed for the television.

"Let's watch a movie."

10:05 PM

"The guy had been knocking over jewelry stores for six months." Marianne said, her eyes on Paul but aware of Rob and Debbie playing darts behind him, at the end of the room. "Mostly smash and grab, although once he showed a knife when a store manager started to chase after him. Anyway, we're taking lunch, and my partner's sitting in the car while I run in for some stuff I needed. I'm almost at the drugstore when an alarm goes off and this guy comes barrel-assing out of the jewelry store, knocks down two teenagers, and flies off away from me. I yell, 'Stop, police' and take off after him. He was fast, but I was faster.

"So I chase the guy through the mall and into the parking garage. I'm only about twenty feet behind him and closing when he decides since he can't outrun me, he's gonna whoop me. He stopped so abruptly my momentum carried me right in front of him before I could stop, too. Now he figures to get in a quick punch before I can set myself, so he throws a roundhouse."

She paused half-a-second, giving her head a quick shake. "I reacted without thinking, you know? I've had some martial arts training and it just kicked in. I grabbed the arm and used the momentum to pull him forward and off his feet as I twisted. But somehow, as he's flying by me, he reaches out, grabs at me with his free hand and suddenly the front of my shirt is ripped open and one side of my bra is up here."

She ran a finger across her chest from the opening in her v-neck, across the top of her left breast, to her armpit. "Now, the guy is down, but scrambling to get back on his feet, so I pull my weapon and yell 'Freeze asshole.' Well, he looks up, sees the gun, then sees my boob waving in the breeze, and his eyes kind of bug out and start flitting back and forth from one to the other. I swear, despite the adrenaline and being pissed and everything, I almost started laughing."

Paul grinned, but said nothing, not wanting to interrupt her.

"Well, by this time, there's about a dozen civilians watching, so I yell at them to stay back, then order the guy face down on the ground. Holding the gun on him with one hand, I get the cuffs on him with the other. Now I can holster the gun, get myself back into the bra and pull my shirt closed, even though most of the buttons were gone. And as I'm doing that, the civilians start applauding."

Paul was laughing, loving both the story and the easy way in which she was telling it.

"Sure, laugh at the poor cop's embarrassment," Marianne said. "But you haven't heard the best part yet.

"When I ordered him to get on the ground and he was going back and forth between the gun and my boob, you know what the jerk said to me? He said 'Man, I wish I had a camera. Nobody's ever gonna believe this in the joint.'"

By now Paul was howling and it took him a minute to get his voice back. "You're an amazing woman, Mare." He started chuckling again. "I'm sorry, but I can't get the picture of you and the gun and the guy looking at you out of my head. Somebody should put that scene in a movie."

That drew a laugh from Marianne. "Well if you ever write the script, remember to give me credit."

She swallowed some of her beer. "The strange thing was, though, even though it was a little embarrassing while it was happening, I didn't think it was all that big a deal until I started writing the arrest report. Then I had to think about whether to put those details in. Technically,

I'm supposed to, but it was too much to think of the report being copied and passed around for some cheap chuckles, so I said the guy tore my shirt and left it at that."

"And nobody found out?"

"Oh, they found out. When the uniforms arrived, they took statements from the civilians who'd witnessed the arrest. I took a pile of crap from the guys for almost a week. But it was worth it. Catching the guy was a real coup. They couldn't give me a promotion so soon after the last one, but they did ask me if I'd be interested in a special two week training seminar in Boston. I hadn't seen Debbie in almost a year since she took the job here and these seminars are like paid vacations, so I jumped at it."

She paused to take another sip from her beer.

"Hey, ummm, I want to thank you for being so nice tonight. It was obvious you didn't know you'd been set up to baby-sit. Yet you stayed and listened to my stories and had some pretty good ones of your own. You even made me laugh and I really appreciate it."

Paul started to protest. But she cut him off.

"Stop, please. You don't make detective at my tender age without being able to read people and situations. So who is she?"

"Who is who?"

Doing her best to sound like a TV cop, she said, "Hey, I'm asking the questions here. Who's the girl you've been thinking about all night while you've been paying attention to me?"

Paul's grin told her she'd been on target. "Was it that obvious?" he asked. "I'm sorry."

Marianne waved off his apology. "It wasn't obvious at all. Just an educated guess. So, who is she?"

"You really are good at your job, aren't you? I'll have to remember never to commit any crimes in Seattle. Her name is Jillian. I met her this morning in a coffee shop."

"A coffee shop? Good coffee? You know how we cops like our coffee."

"The best in Boston. It's across the common on Tremont Street. Coffey's Coffee."

"You're kidding about the name, right?"

"Nope. It's been in the same location forever. Way before either of us were born. If you go there, try the blueberry muffins."

"I will. Thanks. Now tell me about Jillian."

Paul spent the next ten minutes relating the story of how he and Jillian met, his pursuing her out of the coffee shop, and their lunch date.

When he was done, Marianne's hand was at her cheek, her face and eyes soft with emotion.

"What a great story," she said. "What a great way to meet. So when's the first date?"

"I don't know."

"You don't know?"

"Well, I'd planned to call her when I got home tonight, but, ahh, something came up."

"You mean…"

She abruptly stood up and waved. "Yo Debbie, Rob, over here now."

"Mare, you don't have to…"

"Oh yes I do."

Hearing the tone of her voice, Rob and Debbie hurried back to the table.

"What's wrong?" Rob asked. "Did he…"

Marianne cut him off with a glare. "You are in big trouble, pal."

She turned to Debbie.

"Deb, we have to go. Paul has something important to do and it can't wait any longer."

She turned to Paul, leaned in, and kissed him on the cheek.

"Thank you again." She said. "You were very sweet. Jillian is a lucky girl, even if she doesn't know it yet."

"Jillian? Who's Jillian?" Debbie asked as Paul said goodbye and headed for the door.

"I'll tell you later." Marianne turned back to Rob. "As for you…"

10:45 PM

The windows of Paul's third floor condo on the corner of Charlesgate East and Boylston Street looked out across the busy intersection onto the north end of the Fens, a beautiful and peaceful park of ponds, flower beds, and manicured lawns as well as a running track, basketball court, and a baseball field.

He let himself in, dropped his coat on a chair, and headed for the bathroom.

Man, Marianne was something else. Who knew cops could be so hot? And funny. I really had a good time with her tonight...and she seemed to like me...maybe I shouldn't have said anything about Jillian...but she knew...damn she's a good cop. And there is *something about Jillian...*

Three minutes later, his mind was still racing as he walked back into the living room.

...but there's no way I'm moving to Seattle or she's staying in Boston, so forget about her and call Jillian.

He flipped open his wallet, retrieved a small slip of paper, and held it before him with reverence. On it was written *the number*.

A glance at the clock as he fished his phone from his pocket told him it was 10:50.

Is it too late to call?

He sat on the edge of the recliner, next to the table that held a small lamp. After switching on the light, he studied the clock again for half a minute.

Geez, why am I so nervous?

He jumped up and grabbed a beer from the fridge. After a long pull, he checked the clock yet again as he paced in front of the sink.

Come on, get on with it. She's just a girl. But what if she's sleeping? Will she be upset if I wake her? Maybe I should wait and call her in the morning. Maybe...

"What the hell's wrong with me? This girl's got me so freakin' off-balance I can't think straight. Is this some cosmic joke or something? We've both been going to the coffee shop for years and now, suddenly, there she is, right in front of me, stealing my line. I wouldn't even have noticed her if she hadn't…maybe it is fate or something…damn, she even has me talking to myself!"

He shook his head to clear it.

"Call. Just call her before it gets any later."

His thumb started punching keys.

10:55 PM

Less than 350 yards away, Jillian was saying goodbye to her friends. Her second floor apartment at 1171 Boylston Street was across the Fens from Paul's condo.

"Don't worry," Jenna said as she and Liz donned their jackets. "He'll call tomorrow for sure."

Liz agreed. "For sure. He obviously likes you."

Jillian repeated her earlier contention. "If he calls, he calls. I really don't care one way or the other."

Liz chuckled. "Sure you don't. That's why we spent the past four hours talking about him. 'Cause you don't care one way or the other. HAH! You are so in denial girl. Do you even remember what movie we were watching? This guy has you bad, girl, really bad."

"Bad," Jenna mimicked, laughing, "*really bad.*"

Liz turned the knob and opened the door, but before she could move, the phone began to ring. Jillian made no move to answer it.

"What are you waiting for?" Liz asked. "Go get it. It's probably him."

Jillian stood her ground.

"Well if you won't answer it, I will."

Liz started toward the phone on the table but Jillian rushed by her and grabbed the receiver.

"Don't care one way or the other my ass," Liz muttered, heading back to the door.

Jillian pressed the talk button and said, "Hello?"

"Hi, it's Paul. Please tell me it's not too late to call."

Jillian's face lit up. She pointed to the phone and mouthed 'it's him', then waved goodbye to the girls as they closed the door on their way out.

"Hi. It's not too late. Two of my friends just left."

"Sorry to call so late. I was with Rob â€" remember him from the coffee shop this morning? I got tied up with him after work and just walked in a few minutes ago. I'm glad you're still awake."

"And I'm glad you called. Did the manuscript dry out?"

"Sure. After you left, I took it to the Laundromat and put the wet pages in the dryer."

"You did not!"

"No, not really. But it sounded good, didn't it?"

Jillian laughed and realized she'd been laughing a lot since lunch today.

"Are you like this all the time?"

"Like what?"

"Funny."

Paul thought for a few seconds. "I try. I like to laugh, and I like to make other people laugh. Especially people I like."

"Oh, so you're saying you like me?"

"Yes, I'd definitely say I like you. The big question though, the one on which the future of this whole conversation rests is…" He paused for effect. "…do you like Italian food?"

"It's my favorite."

"Whew. Okay. Everything's fine now. I was really worried. I could never date a woman who didn't like Italian food."

"Really?"

"Absolutely. You see, Italian food is more than just food. It not only nourishes the body, it nourishes the soul. It makes your tonsils dance and your heart sing. It fills your stomach, yes, but it also fills you with a sense of peace and contentment. Especially when accompanied by a couple of bottles of Chianti."

Jillian was laughing again. "My, my. Is it only food, or are you this passionate about everything?"

Paul knew what he would have liked to say, but instead offered, "I think I'll let you discover that for yourself, a little at a time. So, tell me about your friends."

Jillian's eyebrows arched at the unexpected question. "You want to hear about my friends?"

"Of course. If they're over there this late on a work night, I'm guessing they're a big part of your life and someday I hope to meet them, so why not get to know a little about them now. Unless you'd rather not talk about them."

Someday I hope to meet them? Someday I hope to meet them! Does he know what he just said? Is he actually thinking that far ahead? How could he be? We just met.

Jillian thought she should be feeling funny about his self-assurance, his presumption that he'd be around long enough to meet her friends. Instead it made her feel warm inside, peaceful and happy.

What is it about this guy that keeps making me feel so opposite to what I should *be feeling?*

"So you're serious? You really want me to tell you about Liz and Jenna?"

"Of course. I wouldn't have asked otherwise. How did you meet them?"

"Okay then," she said, reclining on the sofa. "I hope you're sitting down.

"Liz is Elizabeth Farrell. She's my oldest friend. We met in the third grade and hated each other until half-way through the fourth grade. Then this pint-sized terror named Eddie Lepage started picking on both of us, so we called a temporary truce so we could figure out a way to get back at him. We schemed for almost a week before deciding on a plan.

"Are you bored yet?"

"Not at all. I love revenge stories."

"I see. Well, one day during recess, I started taunting Eddie until he started to chase me. I ran halfway around the yard, then around the back of the school where Liz was waiting. As soon as he turned the corner, she jumped out and screamed at the top of lungs, which didn't bother Eddie at all, but did get him to stop. That's when she threw a glass of water at the front of his pants, soaking them.

"The two of us ran back out to the yard where all the other kids were playing. When Eddie came around the corner to get us, we started laughing and pointing, telling everyone Liz scared him so much he peed in his pants."

She could hear Paul chuckling softly.

"Eddie's denials were long and loud but to no avail. From that day, until his family moved away the following year, he was known as Eddie LePee."

She heard his chuckles become laughs. "Eddie LePee! That's a riot. I bet his folks moved to save him from the humiliation."

Jillian matched his laugh. "Maybe so. Anyway, with our mission accomplished, we found we had a lot in common and since neither of us could remember why we hated each other, we decided to be friends, instead. That was eighteen years ago."

"Whoa…eighteen years! My oldest friend is Rob and I met him in high school. What about the other one? What's her name?"

"Jenna. Jennafer Williams. Liz and I met her freshman year in college."

"Which school?"

"Boston University."

"Oh! Good school. I went to Tufts."

"That's a pretty good school, too."

"It was close to home. And I got a discount because I lived in Medford. Hmmm…I wonder if they still do that? Anyway, Jenna?"

"She was the third girl in a triple dorm room."

"Holy crap! Three girls in one room? With one bathroom?"

"You have no idea! But anyway, we'd all won scholarships…or rather, the school gave Liz and I scholarships. Jenna got hers by winning some national science contest."

"Wow, she must be pretty smart."

"She sure is. But she's such a goofball you'd never know it outside the lab where she works."

Jillian found herself telling him things about Liz and Jenna, what they did, what they liked, things she might have expected to tell a new girlfriend, but not some guy she'd just met.

"Man, I wish I had a friend like Liz. You two sound

more like sisters than friends."

"I guess we are, really."

"At our age, it's hard to imagine having had a best friend for eighteen years. And speaking of age, if I've done my math correctly, you would be 25?"

"Your math is correct," she replied. "Now, to get your age, how much should I add or subtract from mine?"

"You should add three."

"Twenty-eight! You're twenty-eight? I never would have guessed. I thought you were my age, or younger."

"It's my boyish good looks. They're a curse, really. But it's true, I'm only two years away from the big three-oh. Can Social Security be far behind?"

As the conversation continued, each offered tidbits of information, about work, friends, likes, dislikes; the things two people usually offer up at the beginning of a new relationship.

Paul was charming, constantly making her laugh. Both were so caught up in the dialogue, time flew by.

When Jillian thought to check, she was shocked to see it was well after midnight.

Didn't the phone just ring a few minutes ago?

"You know I was so embarrassed at lunch today, I just wanted to go hide somewhere."

"I remember," he said, chuckling, "but there was no reason to be embarrassed. You were nervous. So was I. Heck, if you hadn't knocked it over, I probably would have. Actually, I was more relieved than anything else."

"Relieved?"

"Sure. After all, I made such a fool of myself this morning, and I had this vision of you as, you know, so cool and calm and detached. I had no idea what to say or do to impress you. I just knew I had to. And when the coffee went flying, and you got all flustered...well, I knew we were okay. I knew you'd laugh at my 'most beautiful' joke and I knew we'd hit it off.

"You knew that? How?"

"I'm not sure. I guess because if you really were the cold, aloof type, you wouldn't have reacted that way to the spill. And to tell the truth, by then I had a feeling, but it was probably more hoping than knowing how you'd react to the joke."

Jillian found herself nodding, pleased that his answers were so honest and unguarded.

"Since we're doing *True Confessions* here, I had planned to come in all cold and aloof, what you were expecting, just to test you. I was really afraid you were playing me and I didn't want any part of it, if that's what it was. Knocking over the coffee and you being so nice about it sort of reset my attitude I think."

"Well I'm very glad it did."

"Me too."

Her eyes flicked to the clock again. "You realize it's way after midnight, and I have to get up for work in the morning."

Paul sighed. "I know. So do I. I just don't want to let go of your voice…"

That warm, comfortable feeling flowed through her again.

"…but I will. So now the moment of truth has arrived. Would you like to go out with me Friday night?"

"No."

There was dead silence on the phone line. Paul's face had drained to a ghostly white. Was she really turning him down?

"I'd *like* to go out with you tomorrow night but I can't because I have yoga class and then dinner plans with some friends. So I guess I'll have to hold out until Friday."

It took a moment for Paul to recover his voice and for the color to return to his face.

"You know you almost gave me a heart attack. Was that…"

"Payback for the joke this afternoon? Yes it was." Jillian laughed. "Still want to go out with me?"

Paul was laughing now as well. "Oh yes. I have a feeling getting to know you will be the most interesting thing I'll ever do."

~~~~~~~~~~~~~~~

Thank you for reading the opening chapter of *Coffee in Common.*

Coffee in Common is available in Print and for your Kindle.

The print version is a 339-page, 6 x 9 inch trade paperback printed on high-quality, cream-colored paper.

Available on Amazon, from your local bookseller, and from the publisher at www.masonmarshall.com

Reviews from Amazon

5 stars Realistic Romance
By Elena J. Berry
This review is from: Coffee in Common (Paperback)

I'm typically not a fan of books where I'm not learning something specific about a subject, but I saw the title of this book and, loving coffee and in search of romance myself, decided to give it a look. I was surprised to find myself fully engaged in the characters and story line immediately and (for the first time) reading a book from beginning to end!
~~~~~~~~~~~~~~~

I found the book to be well written and could easily identify with the characters, settings and situations. Not only did it inspire me to have hope in finding my own romance over coffee (great conversation does occur that way), but my teenage daughters were interested in reading the book as well! It's rare to find a story line where various age groups are interested, yet they found themselves being able to identify with the characters and seing themselves in the next phase of their life experiencing something similar.

I'd recommend this light hearted and enjoyable reading to anyone who is looking to find a pleasurable escape and extend 'kudos' to the writer. A job well done!

* * *

5 stars Great read!
By Zoe
This review is from: Coffee in Common (Kindle Edition)

I was surprised by this book. It was well written and creative. It's not your usual cheesy love story, and I liked the side stories. Read it!

* * *

5 stars Not your usual romance
By K-reader
This review is from: Coffee in Common (Kindle Edition)

I love coffee, so I had to read this when I saw the title.

The prologue hints that this may be based on a true story even though the author says it's not. Either way, it was a great, fun read.

There are several stories woven together and so much goes on, I don't know how to summarize the plot. But it's not like any romance I ever read before. It was almost like reading a movie, if that makes any sense.

The characters are very well developed, so much so that by the end of the book it felt like I was leaving behind friends. The author doesn't have any other books listed but I hope she's working on another one with these characters. I especially would like to read more about Priya and about Jillian's little sister.

Maybe the best thing about the story was the dialogue. It all sounded real, like you were overhearing real people talking.

The only thing I didn't like was the very beginning. It started in a coffee shop, which was okay, but two characters were talking about baseball until Paul met Jillian. It was only two or three pages but it started me off in the wrong frame of mind. But once they met, I loved the rest. It was full of surprises.

* * *

5 stars Coffee in common
By Cathy M.
This review is from: Coffee in Common (Paperback)

I just loved it. A great romance. I especially liked all the detail regarding womans clothing and the food they ate on their first date. Made me hungry! It was an easy read, well written book.

USA
tion can be obtained
ng.com
524
B/164

Printed in the USA
CPSIA information can be obtained
at www.ICGtesting.com
CBHW032347010524
7922CB00010B/164

9 781632 470492